MAKING CONVERSATION

Persephone Book N° 83
Published by Persephone Books Ltd 2009

Reprinted 2015

First published in 1931 by Leonard Stein
with Victor Gollancz

© The Gate Theatre, Dublin

Preface © Rachel Billington 2009

Endpapers taken from a 1931 dress silk in a
private collection

Prelim pages typeset in ITC Baskerville by
Keystroke, Wolverhampton

Printed and bound in Germany by
GGP Media GmbH, Poessneck
on Munken Premium (FSC approved)

ISBN 978 1 903155 738

Persephone Books Ltd
59 Lamb's Conduit Street
London WC1N 3NB
020 7242 9292

www.persephonebooks.co.uk

MAKING CONVERSATION
by
CHRISTINE LONGFORD

✼✼✼✼✼✼✼

with a new preface by
RACHEL BILLINGTON

PERSEPHONE BOOKS
LONDON

PREFACE

✸✸✸✸✸✸✸

A few months ago I sat in the archive room in Tullynally Castle, County Westmeath, Ireland and read the letters my aunt, Christine Trew wrote to her future husband, Edward Longford, the 6th Earl of Longford.

It was 1923. During the university terms, they were both in Oxford, Christine, two years older than Edward, had already taken her degree in Greats, he was just setting out on his. During the holidays he was often at Pakenham Hall (now called Tullynally Castle). He had inherited a title, large estates and land, mostly in Ireland, when his father was killed at Gallipoli in 1915. She was Christine Trew, whose mother lost her husband first on his departure from home when his daughter was three and finally when he, a navy man, was drowned in World War One.

A father dying in the Great War was the least of the bonds between Christine and Edward.

In the archive room, a large airy chamber, originally the nursery, the lovers' letters are bundled up in separate stacks, all written before they were married, since afterwards they never spent a day apart.

✳✳✳✳✳✳✳✳✳✳

Edward removed Christine from a modest home in Oxford where the only income came from paying-guests (not 'lodgers' as Martha Freke insists) to a one hundred-room crenellated and turreted castle. At that time the inside staff included a butler, six house maids and many under-staff plus a dozen or so outside who cared for, among other areas, an eight-acre walled fruit and vegetable garden.

If this sounds like the story of King Cophetua and the Beggar-maid the reality was very different – at least from the hero and heroine's point of view. Christine Trew was no pretty little thing, but a strong-minded 'twenties blue-stocking whose mother had moved to Oxford to make sure her clever daughter won a scholarship to Oxford which, just like Martha, in *Making Conversation*, Christine duly did.

Much of the novel closely reflects Christine's own early life. Like Martha she had grown up in the West Country, a single child with an absent father, precociously clever and educated in part by the student lodgers who lived in her home.

Also in the archive room is a memoir written and typed out by Christine after her husband's death. In it she describes how she started writing during the summer of 1930 when she and Edward and friends were staying at Pakenham Hall. 'At odd times I stayed indoors and wrote the first novel that anybody can write, stories of my past life . . .'

I'll come back to this quotation and the line 'the first novel that anybody can write,' because one of the big questions over Christine Longford as a novelist is not *why* she wrote *Making Conversation* – it was almost an obvious step in the literary group in which she moved – but why, after 1935 and three further novels, she never wrote another.

In the early 1920's, Christine Trew was an undergraduate who made friends with writers like Harold Acton and Sinclair Lewis and went up to London for tea parties with Rose Macaulay, Michael Arlen and Noel Coward. Sinclair Lewis, Christine tells us in her memoir, became enough of a friend to slide down the banisters on a tray – whose banisters she doesn't make clear. He also visited Christine at home where 'we went for a country walk in the Oxfordshire mud and talked about literature. He regretted the absence of fundamentals in modern fiction, Love and Hate, Joy and Sorrow, Hunger and Thirst.' To which Christine adds, with her usual briskness, 'Now they have come back with a vengeance.'

She was also welcomed at Garsington Manor by Lady Ottoline Morrell. 'Garsington', Christine writes, 'was my education on Sundays.' She describes a typical visit: 'Tea at a long table, China tea and cress sandwiches. Then Turkish cigarettes and bull's-eyes, wood smoke and incense in a room with Venetian mirrors and Omega Workshop lampshades. Or we might sit in the garden among peacocks and statues, and listen to Bertrand Russell, Lytton Strachey, EM Forster or WB Yeats. My favourite was Bertrand Russell. We did not interrupt them, or ask them for jobs, but we knew it was the kind of conversation we liked.'

Christine several times notes her plan to write, so that when she takes a disappointing third class degree, possibly due to her mother's illness, she and her friend Flora Grierson (daughter of Professor Grierson) consoled each other by agreeing they wanted to write not teach or become academics. As Christine commented, 'I was prepared to become the secretary of a man of genius, preferably a writer; or if I went to work in an office, it must be a publisher's office. Writing was my line, so I had decided when I edited the school magazine; and in time I would write books myself.'

All this Christine perceived as happening in London. Nevertheless, to Flora's disappointment, she decided to learn shorthand and typing in Oxford. Edward had three more years of his degree there and Edward avoided London. Indeed he did not immediately appreciate Christine because he thought she was 'a London woman'. Their first proper meeting was not a success. 'I talked too much and he talked too little. He thought me formidable and I thought him unsociable.'

Despite this faltering start, the age difference, the class barrier and fairly general surprise and sometimes disapproval, they were soon inseparable. Christine had met her 'man of genius'. Bidding farewell to her early superiority in matters of literature and the world, she ceded to him greater knowledge in everything or everything that truly mattered. She admitted she could never turn him into a tidy man or teach him to dance.

She wrote about him after their marriage when he was searching for an occupation, 'He was not meant to be an extra, a walk-on like me.' Class, money and even Edward's relative good looks may have had something to do with her sense of inferiority. Christine was small, with a *jolie-laide* face at best, combining very large mouth with largish nose and

✳✳✳✳✳✳✳✳✳✳

small eyes while Edward had golden curls and handsome Greek god features. Several times in the memoir she refutes any idea that class differences mattered to her and she quotes Edward as saying that Ireland was a republic now and such things as class had become irrelevant.

Christine's description of the first time she saw Edward is too charming and revealing to resist quoting in full:

> In the autumn of 1921, I was just twenty-one and beginning my last year at Oxford. One dark, wet evening I was walking around the big quadrangle of Christchurch with my friend Charles, an accomplished classical scholar. We had been to a lecture on Roman Gaul. In front of us loomed the shape of a boy in one of those Etonian overcoats now extinct, which were baggy, with velvet collars.
>
> Charles said, 'That's Lord Longford.'
> I said 'Oh, is it?'
> I had no special feelings about lords, for or against. I knew some who were intelligent, and it was the only class-distinction I recognised. I was an intellectual snob.
> Charles said 'I hear he has come up with quite a good reputation from Eton.
> I said 'oh, really?' and we discussed Roman remains in Provence.

Money is always important and Christine regretted that she could not be an heiress as Edward's bride. They were something more important: soul-mates. After initial hesita-

✳✳✳✳✳✳✳✳✳✳

tions, they were recognised as such by Edward's widowed mother and his five brothers and sisters, including my father, Frank Pakenham (later Lord Longford).

They were married in a family-only affair, in July 1925 immediately after Edward finished his final examinations. A year or so later they came to live permanently in Ireland. Ireland was Edward's obsession – he had learned Gaelic at Eton – and soon Christine was as fervid a Republican as him.

By 1927, they had bought a house in Leinster Road, Dublin. According to Desmond Guinness, who came to live in Leixlip Castle in the 1950s, when he first met Christine and Edward, 'it was a huge house but furnished like a monastery with a single light bulb hanging from the ceiling in their bedroom.'

The house, huge even by the standards of the owner of a castle, was entirely dwarfed by the vastness of Pakenham Hall and became an escape route from the responsibilities of running a great estate. From then on, in the words of Thomas Pakenham who now lives at Tullynally, they used Pakenham Hall 'as a weekend cottage', and of course a place for holidays.

During this period both Edward and Christine were feeling their way towards their future. They had a passion for the classics nearly as great as all things Irish – and were both extraordinarily well read. In 1928 Christine published her first book, non-fiction: *Vespasian and Some of his Contemporaries*. It was typical that she felt no need to add the word 'Emperor'. This would seem to be a far cry from *Making Conversation* and her later novels but she has already

✽✽✽✽✽✽✽✽✽✽

perfected her elliptical style, which served her so well in her humorous novels. History, in abbreviation, becomes somewhat indigestible, although her command of the facts never gets in the way of a lively anecdote.

Other enthusiasms kept them very active: Chinese artefacts and design of every sort – hangings, pots and carpets – had a magnetic attraction for them both. Tullynally is still filled with evidence of their buying sprees in European and in Dublin shops. They bought for the sheer pleasure of owning an object they admired, not caring about cracks or inferior quality. They loved Chinese colourings and, like naughty children let loose, painted the dark brown panelling of the castle in brilliant red, blue and green. Even the gates to the walled garden became (and remain) a Chinese red.

But it was Edward's next great enthusiasm which was finally to transform their lives and eventually change Christine's direction as a writer. In 1930 Edward joined Micheál MacLiammóir and Hilton Edwards on the board of the newly formed Gate Theatre. In fact, Edward saved the theatre from closure by writing a very large cheque. He continued to do so for the rest of his life, easily overlooking occasional warnings from his trustees.

In her memoir, Christine writes, 'Edward, we know, thought inherited wealth was a crime . . .' Now he had found a noble cause which gave him intense pleasure and where the money could be directed. Christine summarised this: 'We were stage-struck for life, and our stages were all over Ireland, south of the border.' In the early 1930s, their stage was usually in Dublin. It was only in 1938, when Edward

✸✸✸✸✸✸✸✸✸✸

split with Hilton and MacLiammóir to set up Longford Productions (a touring company for half the year), that the theatre completely enveloped Edward and Christine's life. Nevertheless, Edward's direction was set and Christine's only wish was to follow and serve him.

Her four novels, therefore, *Making Conversation*, *Country Places*, *Jiggins of Jigginstown* (originally a play) and *Printed Cotton* were all written and published between 1930 and 1935. Extraordinarily, there is very little mention of them in her memoir even though she was describing the period up to 1939. There is no mention of the last two novels at all and scarcely any suggestion that the first two were published or that they, in particular, *Making Conversation*, received incredibly good reviews. Towards her death she told her friend, the Irish writer and editor, Terence de Vere White, who noted it, that 'she had abandoned the idea of writing about herself and the book [memoir] was to be about her late husband.' Despite good offers, sight unseen, from three publishers, she never allowed it to be published.

The references to her writing that remain in the memoir nevertheless describe the circumstances and her mood as she took up her pen – at least with the first two novels. Both were written at Pakenham Hall during the summer holidays. 'Friends and family stayed, neighbours were visited, a rock garden created, a pure-bred Hereford bull called Johnston Robin purchased.' In Christine's words, 'At odd times I stayed indoors and wrote the first novel that anybody can write, stories of my past life; and here I must say in praise of Edward that he neither stopped it nor censored it. I showed it to him in sections and waited to see if he laughed at the jokes, but I didn't ask for advice and he gave me none, and I showed it to no one else.'

At this point feminists may be grinding their teeth. But it would be to misunderstand the strength of Christine's modesty. She goes on to report tranquilly how a friend guesses 'her secret' and tells her 'to persevere', 'I was doing no harm, and I liked doing it, didn't I? Yes, I certainly did.'

During the summer that she wrote her second novel, *Country Places*, new visitors came to stay, some of them young men like Anthony Powell (her future brother-in-law) and Evelyn Waugh who were already highly regarded writers, others, like John Betjeman, were soon to become famous. Another brother-in-law was the painter of Lytton Strachey, Henry Lamb. The atmosphere was intensely literary and artistic.

Christine paints a vivid picture of this scene and her own modest role in it: 'None of us seemed to be working except Henry [he was painting portraits of the family]. We were on holiday. Still it was easy to disappear at odd times, and we wouldn't know if John was writing a "pome" in his room. Evelyn would come down to breakfast with a determined face and enquire "Who's got any funny letters this morning?" That was the professional writer, keen on the scent, and we handed them over as a solemn duty. He read rapidly and handed them back, the material was stored for the future. We were all glad to make Evelyn laugh. He was kind about my first novel, and now I was doing a second one set in this country, Ireland for ever, as England was off my mind.'

✽✽✽✽✽✽✽✽✽✽

Set against the 'professional' Waugh who was 'kind' about *Making Conversation,* it is easy to see how Christine's sense of her second place category was confirmed. Her own needlepoint wit was outfaced by Waugh's rapier thrusts or Powell's weightier characterisation.

All the same, it seems strange that the reception of *Making Conversation* made so little impression on her. Nine reviews are quoted in the preliminary pages of *Country Places* which followed it. Here are a few: 'One of the wittiest books published for a very long time.' James Agate. 'A first novel of exceptional wit and originality.' Harold Nicholson. 'As funny as anything I've read in a very long time.' LP Hartley. 'I have been going about lately reading extracts from this delicious book to anybody who would lend me his ears.' Compton Mackenzie. For most writers, these were reviews to last a lifetime.

It is true that after *Making Conversation* Christine permanently shifted the background of her novels to Ireland but the same keen eye for human foibles and even keener ear for dialogue dissects the Anglo-Irish landed gentry. It is the area inhabited by Molly Keane who was rediscovered in the 1970s after being modestly published as MJ Farrell in the 1930s. Clever women wrote novels – Pansy Lamb, Christine's sister-in-law wrote novels – but they did not make a big thing of it.

John Cowell, a later friend of Christine's, wrote a biography of the Longfords called *No Profit but the Name*. In it, he quotes Martha Freke's line, 'Men can enjoy themselves without women but women can't enjoy themselves without men', and comments that Christine thought men more intellectual than women. More important still, she had found an intellectual man she adored and deeply admired.

Compton Mackenzie, one of her biggest fans, reviewed *Country Places* in the *Daily Mail*. 'She is a kind of Jane Austen with shingled hair and a cigarette between her lips ... The possibilities of her future as a writer seems to me immense, and I shall open every new book of hers that come my way with the confident hope that she will never make me regret that so early in her career as a novelist I have rashly mentioned her name in the same sentence as Jane Austen's.

But Jane Austen was not married. Edward's demands on Christine were total and she was his willing acolyte. When Edward started writing plays, she too began a play. 'I copied Edward. When I had finished my novel, I had to write a play too.' It was set in Rome and, according to Christine herself, 'mildly funny and not very good.' But Edward wanted plays for the Gate and she obligingly produced over twenty, all performed, none that I have read much better than the first, some worse. Her attempt at a 'commercial play' as she described it, was quite a lot worse.

Many of the plays were adaptations; one, for example, of Maria Edgeworth's novel, *The Absentee*. (Maria Edgeworth had lived near Pakenham Hall and had been friends of the family.) Another, ironically, was of Austen's *Pride and Prejudice*. Some were history plays. None have lasted. Most probably the form did not encourage her wonderfully sardonic sense of humour which makes the novels such a delight.

✳✳✳✳✳✳✳✳✳✳

Repertory theatre had a voracious appetite for new work. Both Edward and Christine were always working at top speed, not only writing, but in later years managing the company. Edward did the designs and costumes, Christine did everything. Their winter touring programme took them to small towns like Cavan, Mullingar, Athlone, Cork, Waterford, Carlow, Drogheda, Kilkenny, Clonmel, Sligo, in the worst of the weather.

Contemporaries describe watching productions back at the Gate summer season. Christine sat with the glazed look of someone who would rather be somewhere else. Edward sat on the edge of his seat, eyes shining, enthusiasm undiminished. Certainly there was no time for novels. Nor, sadly, was there any sign of the two children that, in her memoir, Christine admits that they hoped for.

Still, Christine remained utterly devoted to Edward, a minister to his every need. Unfortunately one of his needs was to consume a mountainous amount of food. By the late 1950s, the handsome, golden-haired youth she had fallen in love with had become spectacularly overweight. Indulgent at first, too late she tried to call a halt to the deadly intake. But any reduction in the potato mountain on his plate caused a major tantrum.

In 1961, when Edward was fifty-nine years old, he died from a massive stroke. Christine, still curiously unchanged in appearance from her 1920s days, the cigarette always in her hand, the 'huge' mouth producing amusing and clever conversation, lived till 1980. At first her days were very busy. She worked still at the Gate, now once again with Edwards

✽✽✽✽✽✽✽✽✽✽

and MacLiammóir, where she became a familiar figure in the box office and ran the accounts, according to Desmond Guinness, who was a trustee, on the back of a Christmas card. She became a distinguished reviewer for the *Irish Times*; among the Tullynally archives are thank you notes from writers such as Patrick Leigh Fermor. But she never wrote another novel.

As time passed, she became prone to depression and spent time in hospital. In her obituary in the *Irish Times*, Hilton Edwards who had seriously fallen out with Edward, wrote 'Her adoration of her husband, Lord Longford, was unmistakable. He appeared to be both husband and child, and the fulfilment of ambition.'

Some time later, Valerie Pakenham found herself talking about Christine with Micháel MacLiammóir. 'If Christine hadn't married that dreadful man, she'd have been the Jane Austen of Ireland' hissed MacLiammóir.

But 'that dreadful man' was Christine's idol. She deeply admired his life-long commitment to promoting Irish theatre and to supporting everything Irish, including freedom and hand-woven tweeds. In her view and the view of many Irishmen – at his funeral, the mourners stretched out of the church and down the streets – he was a great man.

As a novelist myself, I regret that she allowed her talent to be diverted, but at least we have *Making Conversation* – reprinted once before, in 1971, after Pamela Hansford Johnson raved about it in the *Times Literary Supplement*. And in the rather grim atmosphere of early twenty-first-century fiction, even Christine's last three novels provide a refreshingly

✳✳✳✳✳✳✳✳✳✳

light-hearted alternative. I laughed out loud more during my third reading of *Making Conversation* than I have reading any comic novel written over the last thirty years.

In its comment on youth and growing up, it goes far further than providing a witty picture of the times. Martha Freke with her combination of romantic yearnings and sharp-eyed, cold sober criticism is a brilliant portrait of a young woman whose life is about to change.

The novelist with whom Christine Longford can most easily be compared is Nancy Mitford, who continues to be read and admired. This new publication of *Making Conversation* will give another generation a chance to enjoy a truly original and yet mostly forgotten talent.

Rachel Billington
Dorset, 2008

CHAPTER I

"HERE is a little present for you, Ellen," said Martha Freke. "We got it on the pier."

Ellen, the cook-general, undid the wrappings, which revealed a small cardboard box, and in it, on a bed of cotton wool, a brooch which said "Ellen," in bright gold, written in a cursive hand, with a line below it and a full stop after it. "It will help her to remember," Mrs. Freke had said; for Ellen had been christened "Beatrice," which was an unsuitable name for a cook-general, and had to be dropped.

"Isn't it lovely?" asked Martha.

"It's sweet pretty, miss," answered Ellen in the Wessex dialect.

"Yes, it's real gold, too, and they were making them up in any name. And only sixpence each!"

Martha could not understand why her

Making Conversation

mother was frowning and shaking her fist behind Ellen's back.

" I'm sure I'm very much obliged," said Ellen, " no matter what it did cost," and went out.

" You little idiot," said Mrs. Freke. " Now she won't think anything of it. People like that don't, if you tell them the price. Never do it again."

This was the sort of thing that happened, thought Martha, after a really nice day. She had absorbed all the sights of Compton-on-Sea: shopping in the morning, lunch in the Geisha Café, where the mock-turtle soup had a taste unknown at home, and an afternoon on the pier, where they bought the brooch and listened to Braun's band. The conductor was called Herr Braun; and in Martha's mind, " Hair " was an honorific title of mysterious importance. He was a famous conductor in Germany, said her mother, and it was only because he was especially fond of Compton that he consented to come there every summer. Anyway, the day had been

Making Conversation

delightful, and there had been no need to make conversation ; but as usual, as soon as she had opened her mouth unnecessarily, there had been a disaster.

" You should encourage Martha to talk more," said Miss Pilkington, their permanent paying-guest, " or she will be at a disadvantage when she goes out into the world. Of course, it is difficult with an only child." Her manner suggested that if she had been married she would have found it her duty to have at least ten. She was a tall woman with a high complexion, of whom everyone said they thought she must have been handsome once ; and she made a point of being sensible. That was why she had to pay to be a guest. She had an extensive knowledge of Switzerland ; and to Martha she was an interpreter of the outside world, which was evidently an unpleasant place.

" How are you getting on with your music, Martha ? "

After a pause, " I don't know, Miss Pilkington."

Making Conversation

" Well, you must hurry up and get ready to play my accompaniments. You know, it's a very useful thing for a girl to be able to do, later on."

Almost every evening they had a little music. Mrs. Freke played, and Miss Pilkington stood by the piano in a black evening dress, square at the neck, and with little net sleeves. She clasped her hands over her stomach, and a great volume of low-pitched sound came out. There was a French song about a " *Belle, belle nuit de mai,*" and it ended, " *Te souviens-tu, ma bien-aimée !* " All her songs were supposed to be sung by men to ladies. There were some very noisy ones called " The Herricks," with accompaniments which went all over the piano. " Bid me to live, And I will live, Thy protestant to be." Martha connected that with Miss Pilkington's regular attendance at church. It was not among the hymns and sacred songs which were confined to Sundays, but it was much more stirring to the religious emotions than " Oh, rest in the Lord," and the little bits

Making Conversation

from oratorios, which they were always trying to find, in books bound in two shades of brown.

When there were a lot of paying-guests, Martha used to come in and recite poetry. This she preferred to conversation, as she had a good memory, and was willing to take all the credit for the works of Lord Tennyson and Longfellow and Lord Macaulay. She learned to speak slowly and distinctly, as the paying-guests were sometimes old and deaf. Her mother used to hear her recitations in private, and tell her what action to put into them. They usually went well; except once when the chaplain of the Consumptives' Sanatorium came to tea. He was a very old man, and had been sent there after several other chaplains had caught consumption and died, because the sanatorium was rather old-fashioned. Martha began:

" 'The Famine,' from Longfellow's 'Hiawatha.' 'Oh, the long and dreary winter! Oh, the cold and cruel winter! Ever thicker, thicker, thicker, Froze the

Making Conversation

ice on lake and river, Ever deeper, deeper, deeper. . . . ' "

But she did it much too quickly, like a gramophone record which has been put on at the wrong speed; and when she stopped breathless, the applause was less striking than usual. The entertainment had taken only half the requisite time; and it left an opportunity for the kind of conversation she hated.

" Do you go to school, my dear ? "

" Yes, Mr. Beauchamp, I go to the High School."

" Oh, yes, a very good school. And do they make you work very hard ? "

" Yes, they do rather."

" Very wise, too," said Miss Pilkington. " These new theories of education make the children think life is all a game. And when they grow up, they find it is not."

" I think it is one of the High Schools," said Mr. Beauchamp, " in which the Duchess of Albany is interested."

" No, it isn't one of those," said Martha,

Making Conversation

in a loud eager voice ; " I think it was once, but now it isn't any more."

There was a silence, which was broken by Mrs. Freke. " Miss Spencer has her enemies," she said, " and she has a temper, but there is no doubt she is a good teacher."

" And how is the cricket club ? " asked Mr. Beauchamp.

" They don't play cricket," shouted Martha.

" Dear, dear ! Then what do we play ? "

" I don't play anything ! "

" Such a pity," said Miss Pilkington.

" I believe the Close School is very good, too," said Mr. Beauchamp.

" But the type of child there is inferior," said Mrs. Freke. " And Miss Spencer gives more individual attention."

" It is very important," said Miss Pilkington, " especially for a girl, not to pick up the wrong kind of friends."

" And to speak the Queen's English," said Mr. Beauchamp. " There is not a trace of Somerset in your little girl's accent."

Making Conversation

" I should hope not ! " said Mrs. Freke.

Miss Pilkington had first come to her in answer to an advertisement : " Board residence. Officer's wife receives few guests in country home, Wessex. Delightful surroundings, fishing, tennis. Musical. Pukka sahib. Terms moderate, lower to permanency."

This was mostly true. The military connexion grew fainter with the years. It was some time since Major Freke had written too many cheques, and disappeared. He was now thought to have become nautical, and to be interested in salvaging ships. But he had left his mark on the decoration of Hillview: big peacock-feather fans behind the piano, ebony elephants on the mantelpieces, and two tables covered with Indian brass in the drawing-room.

Hillview was a square house with six bedrooms, one bathroom, a dining-room, a drawing-room, a breakfast-room, and a smoking-room where no one smoked. When there were male visitors, they smoked, according to the advanced custom

Making Conversation

of the period, in the drawing-room. If the house was full of paying-guests, the one bathroom was inadequate ; so was Ellen the cook-general, and another girl came in from the village. The house was in the main street of the small village of Coombe, which was three miles from Adderbury, the town where Martha went to school, and where there were cheese-factories, a jam-factory and a shoe-factory. There were hills behind Coombe, where Miss Pilkington sketched ; and there was certainly one tennis-court at Hillview, and a stream at the end of the garden.

The hills were called the Knoll, the Round House Hill, Tylee's Hill, Tor Hill and the Lion Hill. The Round House was a disused shooting-box, and the Tor a ruin ; Tylee's belonged to Mr. Tylee, a big farmer ; and the Lion Hill was where some remains of a prehistoric animal had been discovered. That made it the most interesting, or rather the least dull, of all of them, because one might find some more bones. On Tylee's Hill grew the best

Making Conversation

mushrooms and blackberries, but it was supposed to be trespassing to take them. Mr. Tylee, who was a little mad, used to lie on the ground with a gun and wait for poachers; and though he could easily spare a few blackberries, it was as well to be on the safe side. The Round House Hill was famous for adders, and Martha once saw one among the loose stones around the house.

"What a big worm," she said to her mother and Miss Pilkington.

"Adder! Quick!" said Mrs. Freke, and killed it with several stones. What a brave woman she was; and Martha was not frightened at the time, but was terrified later, when her mother told the story.

"There it was, a long white thing, not so very long really, but white and wriggling, with a v for viper on its head, and Martha was just going to step on it." That was not strictly true, as Martha never trod on worms; she was too fastidious; and she had not noticed its initial.

"Is it called a viper in every language?" she asked.

Making Conversation

"Practically every language," answered her mother without hesitation.

"It is *vipère* in French," said Miss Pilkington, which seemed to prove it. Martha also connected adders with Adderbury; and from that time she loathed the Round House Hill. Snakes and wasps provided her with her first religious doubts, as she could not believe they were made by God.

The terms at Hillview were moderate, as the advertisement said; and Mrs. Freke sometimes feared that she must be keeping the paying-guests for nothing. But Miss Pilkington was satisfactory, since she paid in advance, in a discreet envelope, and ate very little. She brought in a nett profit of ten or fifteen shillings a week.

Sometimes the vicar sent a surplus pupil or two to board with Mrs. Freke, and for that and other reasons she was among his few supporters in the parish. The Rev. Andrew Pyggott was a man of charming appearance, between fifty and sixty years

Making Conversation

old, with curly grey hair and a well-preserved complexion. But long ago the truth about him had been revealed, that he retained the Fellowship of an Oxford college on the condition of celibacy. This had a disastrous effect on the numbers of the congregation, which, as is usual in country parishes, was largely composed of women. He was said to be a distinguished scholar, and had pupils in his house whom he prepared for Oxford and Cambridge. These were among the social advantages of Hillview, and Mrs. Freke called them "the boys." Some were sent to learn the language and social customs of England, as well as Latin and Greek. There were South Americans with diamond tie-pins, who could not drink water, because it made them bilious; and Mauritians, who were a puzzle in geography, and incredible as belonging to "our Empire," because they spoke French; but they made up for that by their whole-hearted appreciation of English tailoring. And of course there were Americans, who made less progress in

Making Conversation

English than any other race, and could not stay in the same house as Japanese.

When the family of Xenophon D. Peck made that clear, Mr. Pyggott sent Mr. Murate and Mr. Yoshikawa to Mrs. Freke. She asked Miss Pilkington if she had any objections.

" Not at all," said Miss Pilkington, who was broad-minded. " After all, their civilisation is older than ours."

" Yes," said Mrs. Freke vaguely, " and they're quite different from Indians."

They were not much taller than Martha, and the crowns of their little felt hats were pinched in a Continental fashion. Martha asked them about Tokyo. " Very nice town," said Mr. Yoshikawa. " Many large department stores exactly same like Selfridge's."

" Have you a nice house there ? "

" Very nice house. Mr. Murate has two houses."

" I have two houses," said Mr. Murate, " two banks, two grand pianos, two Daimler motor-cars."

Making Conversation

The first evidence of the clash of civilisations was when Martha found Mr. Murate clapping his hands at a spider. We all know that, in books, children clap their hands with glee; and though Martha doubted if she had ever experienced an acute sensation of glee, and had never wanted to clap her hands, she was interested in this display.

" Do you like spiders ? " she asked him.

" I can't bear them."

" Japanese gentlemen," said Mr. Murate, " no like."

" You don't like ? Then why do you clap your hands ? "

" Japanese gentlemen no like, Japanese gentlemen clap hands."

Then there was the time they had a leg of lamb and mint-sauce for lunch on Easter Sunday, and Japanese gentlemen didn't like it.

" In India," said Mrs. Freke, " there are people who won't eat beef, and people who won't eat pork. But I have never heard of people not eating lamb ! We consider it a delicacy," she said firmly.

Making Conversation

"The Emperor Gaius did not," said Mr. Spicer, the curate, who was boarding with them at the time. "So we gather from Philo the Jew of Alexandria." He repeated in a loud voice to the Japanese: "Gaius, or Caligula, the mad Roman emperor, did not like lamb."

Mr. Murate was sulky, hungry and unimpressed, but Mr. Yoshikawa resented the imputation that they were mad. "Japanese gentlemen not like mutton. In Europe everyone like mutton. Japanese gentlemen say, in Europe everyone smell exactly same like mutton. Poof!" And he made a gesture as if waving an unpleasant smell from his nostrils.

Another time, someone used the abbreviation "Jap" by mistake; and the two Japanese gentlemen got up and went to their bedrooms on principle, and did not reappear for about a quarter of an hour.

"And you must never, never say 'Mikado' to them," said Mrs. Freke to Martha, who found the perils of conversation were increasing beyond belief. She

Making Conversation

was not sorry when the Japanese gentlemen left them for a clergyman's family, because, " in clergyman's family you have sewing-parties," and they enjoyed that more than music in the evenings.

CHAPTER II

MARTHA used to drive into Adderbury five days a week to school, in a hired waggonette which belonged to Mr. John Humphreys. He was a dark silent man of about fifty, with a drooping black moustache, who was a Plymouth Brother. He had been in Canada in his youth, and had been cured of paralysis by a faith-healer in Montreal. He drove Martha only as far as the station, where he met the nine o'clock train, and fetched the morning papers and some parcels. This meant that she had to walk up the long High Street, and always missed prayers at school and was late for the first lesson. She had to start early enough, goodness knows, and it was horrible in the winter, getting up by candle-light and sheltering from the rain under an oilcloth sheet in the open waggonette. All the way up the street she used to smell the frying bacon and eggs of

Making Conversation

those inhabitants who lived under and over their shops ; and combined with the usual apprehension of school, it made her feel sick.

On Mondays, Wednesdays and Fridays, the first lesson was religious knowledge, taken by Miss Spencer, the headmistress, herself. The whole school of twenty-four pupils joined in it, and the red felt curtains which divided the schoolroom in two were pulled back. There were nominally five forms in the High School : twelve little girls in the Third Form, eight between the Fourth and Fifth Forms, and four called the " Little Ones," who were the Second and First Forms and the Kindergarten combined. The last were taught at the Boarding House across the road by Miss Gloria Grossmith, Miss Spencer's partner. The Third Form mistress was Miss Jenkins, whom the children called " Mad Jenkins," because once she had thrown a pile of exercise-books at Miss Spencer's head. The higher forms were taken by Miss Spencer ; and French and drawing were taught by Mademoiselle Perrels, who

Making Conversation

was really a Boer, and had been taken on at a reduced salary during the Boer War.

This was the September of 1911, at the beginning of the Autumn Term, when Martha was almost eleven and in the Third Form. She was good at everything except nature study and French conversation, the latter because she hated conversation of any kind, and the former because she preferred theory to experiment. The *Look About You Nature Book* was the most stupid text-book they had in the school ; and by the time she had walked down the High Street every afternoon to meet the waggonette, trundled home and had tea, she had no eye for the natural beauties of Coombe. So she always did her " nature " homework out of her head. It was the Monday after she had been to Compton-on-Sea on Saturday. She hardly looked at the new autumn hats in the windows of Pavey & Son, Adderbury's premier drapers, or at the so-called Peter Pan collars in the window of Mrs. Knight, the other draper, but hurried into the side door of the High School. The front door

Making Conversation

was never opened except to visiting parents and for prize-givings ; and once there had been a brass plate on it, which had been removed and left a mark.

The cloak-room had a strong smell of rubber and sweat, and was full of stiff straw hats with red ribbons, coats mostly mackintosh, red shoe-bags and goloshes. Martha hung her grey mackintosh and her straw hat on a peg marked " M. Freke," put on some brown slippers out of her bag, and laid some brown goloshes ready for lunch-time. Everyone had to wear goloshes over their slippers when they went from the School to the House. They were of every size, but all black except hers, and many were torn, split and peeling. There was a small mirror over a water-basin, and Martha combed her hair, which was curly and of a nondescript shade, and tied her black velvet band tight round her head. Her face gave her most satisfaction when observed directly from the front, as she had a rather receding chin ; and she looked soulfully into the mirror, to make

Making Conversation

her eyes appear as big as possible. " What a pity the child has such small eyes," one of the paying-guests had once observed in her hearing ; " but perhaps they will grow." She pulled up a navy-blue serge skirt, showing a stiff, clean, white petticoat, and pulled down a clean white shirt-blouse ; and then she went upstairs. Outside the door of the class-room, she had the usual feeling of cerebral paralysis, but gave herself courage by remembering she was good at recitation, and cleverer than most of the girls in the school. She recited to herself for a fraction of a second some lines of Lord Macaulay which she found inspiring, though vague in sense : " Now, by the shades beneath us, And by the gods above, Add not unto your cruel hate, Your *Yet More Cruel Love* ! " She put her head around the door, and looked to the end of the long, low room.

" This is a room to dream in," said visiting parents, though the children knew better. It had an uneven floor, and beams in the ceiling, and some of the windows had

Making Conversation

diamond panes. There was supposed to be a ghost in it at night. Just once Miss Spencer sent one of the boarders up to it after dark, with a lantern. It was Elsie Brace, a big girl with a long skirt, and hair plaited into what was called a " doorknocker," the next stage to putting it up ; and she was sent to fetch some exercise-books she had forgotten. But she screamed and yelled, until people collected in a crowd outside, and the policeman came and fetched her back.

At the end of the room, standing behind a desk, was a tall woman with prominent eyeballs, dilated nostrils, and soft, thick lips. She was wearing a white shirt-blouse, with a stiff white collar and a man's tie, and a black skirt cut very tight over the waist and hips. Her voice was loud but pleasant, and she was just asking, " Now, which of the two do you think is more to be envied ? "

There was a flutter among seven rows of little girls, sitting in white blouses and dark blue skirts at yellow pitch-pine desks.

Making Conversation

Two rows of three for the Fourth Form in front; then the two Fifth Form girls, who were joint heads of the school, and were called " consuls," because of Roman history. A gap, and then the " Little Ones," sitting close together, with Miss Grossmith near them listening. At the back of the room was the amorphous Third, which Martha hoped to reach without being noticed. But, " Ah, here is somebody's nose again!" said Miss Spencer, curling her lips back from her gums in a smile. " Several minutes before Martha comes into the room, we see her nose!"

There was a faint titter led by Miss Grossmith.

" Now, Martha, do you remember how *I* come into a room?"

" No, Miss Spencer."

" Watch me, next time you have the opportunity. It is never too early for a woman to learn to be graceful. One day, when you grow up, you will catch sight of yourself unexpectedly in a long mirror, in a shop-window, for instance, and you will have no

Making Conversation

one but me to thank if you find you have a decent shape."

"Yes, Miss Spencer." (Always this insistence on the unpleasant future.)

"Now, I have just been telling the school that this morning I received two letters from old pupils. One was from a girl who had been chosen to play hockey for the county, and the other from a girl who was engaged to be married. Now, which of them should I congratulate more?"

Both subjects seemed to Martha remote in interest. It was only necessary to divert Miss Spencer's attention from herself, so she chose the less controversial answer, as it seemed.

"The one who was going to play hockey."

The effect was disappointing. "Why?" asked Miss Spencer, tapping the desk with a ruler, and making the india-rubber jump.

"I don't know."

"Is your mother going to let you play net-ball this term?"

Making Conversation

" No, Miss Spencer."

Miss Grossmith laughed, and so did the two consuls.

" Why not ? "

" She doesn't like me to stay late."

" I am very sorry for you, Martha, in more ways than one. Now we must get on with our divinity lesson. What is the right method of interpreting the Commandments ? "

Several hands shot up. " Gertrude Harris," said Miss Spencer, pointing a pencil at a little girl with red hair.

" Not only in the letter, but in the spirit."

" Quite right. And now, what is the next one ? "

Hands went up from everyone except the " Little Ones."

" Millicent Evans."

" Thou shalt not commit adultery."

" Quite right. And how do we interpret this ? "

There was a pause. Both the two consuls were suddenly very busy taking notes, with

Making Conversation

their heads bent low over their exercise-books. They were big girls with their hair in door-knockers, tied with stiff bows of black ribbon. Clarice Crease, the popular one, had dark hair and a slight moustache, and Ruby West had red hair, a red face, gold-rimmed spectacles and gold wires over her teeth.

"Now, Martha," said Miss Spencer, "what is adultery?"

Martha had not the faintest idea. "It is a sin," she said, "committed by adúlts," putting the accent on the second syllable.

"That is a parrot's answer. You think you are very clever, Martha, attempting to conceal your ignorance and your lack of thought. The attempt at concealment is no better than a lie. Adultery is self-indulgence. It is the extra lump of sugar in your tea. It is the extra ten minutes in bed in the morning. It is the extra five minutes a little girl wastes by dawdling up the High Street and gaping at the shop-windows. It is the time we spend on looking at ourselves in the mirror and fluffing out our hair. It is the

Making Conversation

lust of the flesh and the pride of life, and if we give way to it ever so little, it leads us to destruction."

Martha settled down at her desk, knowing she would not be asked any more questions in the same lesson. At ten o'clock Miss Spencer slapped a bell, and two girls called "monitors," with red rosettes safety-pinned to their blouses, rushed out and pulled the curtains which cut off the Third Form.

Miss Jenkins arrived to give an English lesson. She was tall and blonde, with an elaborate coiffure, and opinion about her was divided. All the Harrises, who were boarders, thought her sweet, and Gertrude had a G.P., or "*grande passion*," for her; but Martha found her dull. The only qualification Miss Jenkins had for teaching English was that she was of Welsh extraction, and there was not much opening for her at home. When she lost her temper, she remembered her patriotism, and called Miss Spencer " disgusting English."

" I have your compositions to give back," said Miss Jenkins. There were the

Making Conversation

usual spelling and grammar mistakes. Edith Brookes, who was abnormally fat, and still in the Third Form although she was sixteen, had her composition returned to be done again. "It is unintelligible," said Miss Jenkins. "The same to you!" said Edith grinning, and making an inspired guess at the meaning of the word. She then put out her tongue. "Edith," said Miss Jenkins, "either you apologise or leave the room at once."

Edith walked slowly out, rolling her fat hips in a way which the Third Form found irresistibly funny. She went downstairs to the cloak-room, and amused herself mixing up the goloshes. It was not the first time this had happened.

Martha smugly awaited her own composition, which she knew to be free of spelling and grammar mistakes. It began and ended with a quotation, and the subject, which was "Patriotism," lent itself to her style.

> *"Breathes there a man with soul so dead*
> *Who never to himself hath said,*
> *'This is my own, my native land'?*

Making Conversation

" Patriotism, or love of country, is the noblest emotion known to man. It was patriotism which made many brave men give their lives for their country in the *Iliad* and the *Æneid*, the Greek and Roman Epics, the Battle of Hastings, the Battles of Agincourt and Crecy, the Indian Mutiny, the Crimea and the Boer War. It is patriotism which makes us brave the heat and cold, in every part of the globe. We can all be patriots. Children at school can do their share, like Lord Kitchener at the head of his Army. Women can be as patriotic as men, and even more so.

> *What have I done for thee,*
> *England, my England?*
> *What is there I would not do?*
> *England, my own!*

" On the other hand, ' What do they know of England, who only England know ? ' Travel broadens the mind, and it is only when we travel that we become true patriots.

Making Conversation

"In conclusion, Doctor Johnson said, 'Patriotism is the last refuge of the scoundrel.'"

Miss Jenkins had this exercise-book in front of her, and Martha recognised her own handwriting even upside down.

"Martha, your composition is not so good as usual."

"What nonsense," thought Martha; this dull woman did not appreciate style. "Wasn't it, Miss Jenkins?"

"No, it was too disconnected. It begins well, but goes off towards the end. Now, children, I have often told you to put quotations in your compositions, but you must see that they fit in nicely. Martha, where did you get your last quotation?"

"Out of the quotation dictionary."

Martha felt bored and lonely, surrounded by members of the Third Form who showed her no sympathy, because usually she had high marks for composition and could afford to miss a few.

At 10.45, she always ran over to the

Making Conversation

House for a glass of bluish milk, which she was supposed to need because of her journey, and for which her mother paid. She looked for her goloshes, which were the only brown ones in a welter of black, and should be easily found, but that Edith Brookes had kicked one of them under the basin. As she found them, she heard someone bounding down the stairs, and without looking round, Martha knew it was Miss Spencer.

" Dear, dear, and why must we always be different from the other girls, with our brown goloshes ? "

" All my shoes and stockings are brown, Miss Spencer."

" Oh, indeed, and doesn't your mother know that little girls' legs look much fatter and less workmanlike in brown ? "

" I don't know." In fact, Martha took her mother's authority for granted on such subects ; but when she was not interested in a controversy, she always said she didn't know.

" And what about this mop of hair ? When are we going to plait it ? "

" I don't know." But she knew that it

Making Conversation

was unplaitable. Miss Spencer seized some in her hand and pulled it hard, until Martha's eyes bulged.

"Now run over and drink your milk quickly, and come to my study afterwards. I want to speak to you."

Martha pulled off her goloshes in the dark hall of the House, ran to the kitchen, where she tossed off some cold, thin milk, and then, wiping her mouth, waited outside the headmistress's door.

"Now, child, I want to speak to you about net-ball."

"Yes, Miss Spencer."

"Wouldn't you like to play games with the other girls?"

"I don't know."

"Now, I want to tell you that you are in danger of becoming a very unhappy little girl. Owing to unfortunate circumstances, you are brought up for the most part among grown-up people, and you are losing your childhood."

"Yes, Miss Spencer." Martha was beginning to feel tearful from self-pity.

Making Conversation

"You are lacking in community spirit. The best means of counteracting your mode of life would be net-ball. Tell your mother that one day you will regret the opportunities you have missed."

Miss Spencer had a very wet mouth, which splashed as she spoke. A long-distance splash and the reference to net-ball restored to Martha a sense of reality.

"I have to go home with Mr. Humphreys," she said.

"Nonsense. Some other arrangement could be made. Now, I should like you to understand that you may think you are a clever little girl because you are good at your lessons, but that is not everything. There are many B.A.s of Oxford and Cambridge whom decent people would not be seen speaking to, remember that!"

The next lessons in the Third Form were French verbs and algebra, and gave Martha no trouble. At one o'clock the day-girls went home, and Martha went to the House with the boarders. Five of them were Harrises, and came from a remote suburb of

Making Conversation

London. Their sharp Home Counties accent was considered to counteract the dangers of Wessex dialect in the school. They were all popular and intelligent, and they had great fun in the holidays, watching the traffic on the London–Brighton road. Martha had no G.P.s for anyone, but a dispassionate admiration for Violet Harris, whose hair-ribbon was fixed to her hair with two safety-pins, and who had two combs and two hair-slides as well. Everyone in the Third had some favourite in the Fourth or Fifth.

" What do you think of the Big Girls ? " Martha had been asked in her first term.

" I don't know."

" I like Clarice. Say you like Clarice ! "

" I don't like her," said someone with an original point of view, " I think she's namby."

Anyway, Martha liked the Harrises. One day she said to Gertrude, " My mother says you are Jews. Are you ? "

" Of course not ! " said Gertrude. " Tell her to mind her own business."

Making Conversation

" Aren't you really ? "

" Certainly not. Mother doesn't allow us to know Jews, and that's why we are sent here, because all the schools in London are full of them. You let lodgings, don't you ? "

" Oh, no, we only take in paying-guests."

Edith Brookes was also a boarder, and Ruby West, whose family was in India ; and there were the two little Hills, whose father was a farmer (always referred to as a " big " farmer), who were sent to acquire an accent. Miss Spencer sat at one end of the dining-table, and Miss Grossmith at the other. The children called her " Gloria " behind her back, or sometimes " Mopstick," because she had a large head of hair and a small thin body. Her nose was red, with large pores, and under a coating of powder it looked like a sugared strawberry. Once Martha asked her mother why Miss Grossmith's nose was red. " It is because she has a bad circulation, dear. Nothing is more important than a good

Making Conversation

circulation, and that is why you should take plenty of exercise and run about in the open air, instead of hugging the fire." But perhaps this explanation was not the whole truth, because Mrs. Freke and Miss Pilkington went on talking in low tones, and in the end Mrs. Freke said, " I have certainly never smelled either of them." Martha connected this with another mystery, that of the colour-bar. Her mother said the coloured races had an unpleasant smell, and that was why white people could not mix with them. " There was something else too, wasn't there ? " said Miss Pilkington. " Oh, I never believed a word of that. They are great friends, that's all."

Mademoiselle Perrels was very big and untidy. The first course of the meal was boiled beef and carrots, and even before it arrived, the smell was overpowering. Dishes of blackened potatoes and of brownish greens were passed along the table.

" Now for our French idioms," said Mademoiselle. Everyone had to say a French idiom before they began. Martha

Making Conversation

had one which she thought especially silly: "*Assez pour faire pleurer un chat.*— Enough to make a cat laugh." It was obviously not a good translation. Conversation began about net-ball. The meat was so tough that Martha spat it furtively into her handkerchief, which she then squeezed into her pocket. Pudding was prune-pudding or milk. She could not risk a prune-pudding again, since last term when she had secreted it and put it down the drain, stones and all. The drain had been choked, and the plumber called in, and though she was not discovered, she knew it was her fault. So she said, " Milk, please."

" Milk again, Martha ! " exclaimed Miss Spencer. " Do you know what happens to people who eat nothing but milk-pudding ? "

" No, Miss Spencer."

" Their stomachs grow into such a shape that they can eat nothing else."

After lunch all the children went into the playroom and began whispering in

Making Conversation

groups. Martha attached herself to one group. " Go away," said Mary Spicer; " this isn't your business."

She heard whispers of " goal, goal, half-back, wing," and concluded the secret must be about the team. The other group was in high spirits.

" Go away," said Violet Harris; " you don't know about adultery."

" I do."

" You don't."

" I do."

" You said you didn't this morning."

" You didn't say you did."

" Go away, anyway!"

That evening Martha went into the drawing-room to say good night to Miss Pilkington, who asked her how she had enjoyed school.

" Not very much to-day, thank you."

" Why not, dear?"

" Miss Spencer pulled my hair, and said I had committed adultery."

" Nonsense, dear, you must have misunderstood her."

Making Conversation

" I didn't."

" Don't contradict, dear," said her mother.

Martha enjoyed the luxury of crying in bed. It seemed that conversation was desirable, but conversation often meant contradiction.

CHAPTER III

It was another attempt at conversation that led to Martha's leaving the High School. One day in the Spring Term the boarders were discussing the White Slave Traffic. Marjorie Hill was saying, " Daddy told us never to speak to strangers when we were out for a walk."

" Or to take a lift in a motor-car," said Ida.

" No," said Millicent Harris, the second of the family. " And if anyone tells you your mother has been taken ill round the corner, and tells you to come to the hospital, you mustn't go."

The door opened, and Miss Spencer came in.

" Well, girls, and what have you been gossiping about ? "

" We were just discussing the White Slave Traffic, Miss Spencer," said Marjorie brightly.

Making Conversation

"*What* did you say?" asked Miss Spencer, although she had heard. "Do you know that is an expression I would not take on my lips?"

"No, Miss Spencer?"

"Do you know I would rather say anything to my girls, I would rather say *damn* to them, than that?"

"Oh, Miss Spencer!" said Marjorie, who was shocked.

"Never, never say it again. And get some work to employ your empty little minds."

When she had gone, they put out their tongues, and put their fingers to their noses, a habit which was very common that term.

In the afternoon there was a lecture from the headmistress to the whole school: "Girls, I wish to speak to you all about something which has come to my notice. There is a vile practice afoot in the school, and the sooner it is stamped out the better it will be for the health of the community. You all know what it is. Let each girl's conscience accuse her."

Several girls blushed, and Grace Parsons

Making Conversation

looked as if she were going to faint, which she often did.

" I see guilt written on many faces, and I see surprise nowhere. This is a warning, and I think it will not be without effect."

Martha and Gertrude Harris both made an excuse to leave their preparation and go downstairs, where they talked it over.

" I suppose she meant the White Slave Traffic," said Gertrude.

" Or putting your fingers to your nose. Why shouldn't we talk about the White Slave Traffic? It's very important."

" What I don't see," said Gertrude, " is what they make you do when they've got you."

" Why, they make you commit adultery, of course."

" How did you find out about committing adultery?"

" Out of books, of course. Haven't you read *The Light that Failed* out of the library?"

" Oh, yes!"

" And then we had a paying-guest who

Making Conversation

had a baby who was not right, you know. I heard mother say it was like Topsy in *Uncle Tom's Cabin*. It wasn't very black, but a rather funny colour."

" They don't always go black, do they ? "

" Oh, yes, always. Don't you remember, in the *Wide, Wide World*, the aunt who was slightly black, and always wore a scarf round her neck, because there was a streak ? And the girl in *Adam Bede*, when she was going to have a baby, her mother discovered it when she took her to the dressmaker, because she was going streaky ? "

" I don't believe it's that."

" Of course it is. And we had another paying-guest who came from Jamaica, who told us that you don't meet people who are even slightly black, and sometimes you couldn't possibly notice it."

" But that isn't anything to do with it."

" It is. You never meet people who are like that. It's the same thing with Indians. They always *smell*, too. Some people say Miss Spencer and Miss Grossmith do."

Making Conversation

One of the monitors came down to tell them they had been downstairs long enough, and she gave them each a bad conduct mark for loitering and talking.

The next day, after lunch, there was an animated group in the playroom discussing a secret subject. Edith Brookes was in the centre, and everyone was giggling and displaying surprise. Martha attached herself to the outskirts.

" What's a locum ? " asked one of the little Hills.

" It's a locum tenens," said Edith, who was rarely in a position of intellectual superiority. " Someone who does the doctor's work when he is away."

That evening Martha's mother was brushing her hair, and Miss Pilkington was watching. (" Nice hair," she said, " and a good skin are a great standby to a girl.")

" What did you do in the dinner-hour to-day, dear ? " asked Mrs. Freke. " Have you got a book ? "

" Oh, yes, I have *The Fifth Form at St.*

Making Conversation

Dominic's. It's lovely. But it isn't so good as *The Rank Outsider*."

" Aren't there any girls' school stories in the library ? "

" Yes, there are, but no one likes them, they're too namby. And we talk a lot, too."

" What were you talking about to-day ?"

" Oh, various things. It was mostly Edith Brookes." There was a silence, during which Martha felt she was being drawn out, and had better go on. " She was telling us about how she committed adultery with the local demon."

Mrs. Freke pulled her hair, and told her to say good night quickly, though the brushing was not finished. Next morning she had to take a note from her mother to Miss Spencer, and at eleven o'clock Miss Spencer sent for her.

She tapped at the study door with the usual feeling that she called a dentist-feeling, because one had it in a dentist's waiting-room. Lately she had it before recitations, too, though she never had

Making Conversation

when she was smaller. She wondered what this must be about; it must be net-ball.

" Come in ! " sang Miss Spencer, in the resonant, carrying voice which she recommended the school to imitate. (" You must learn to sing your words, and that will help your enunciation.") Martha walked into the room, which she knew and feared. There was something sinister about the comparative comfort of the furniture : a sofa with a Paisley shawl draped over it, two armchairs, a little chair upholstered in green velvet, a writing-desk and some small tables. Behind the sofa was the Collard & Collard piano, where she had music-lessons with Miss Spencer, who rapped her knuckles with a gold pencil. There were photographs on the mantelpiece, of Miss Spencer's brother who had a private school in the east of England, and of Miss Grossmith's family, who had Indian connexions like Martha's. That must account for the ebony elephants, just like the ones at home.

Making Conversation

" Now, Martha, I want to speak to you very seriously."

" Yes, Miss Spencer."

" Do you know what it is about ? "

" No, I don't," said Martha, and began to giggle slightly.

" Hold on ! " said Miss Spencer in a loud voice, as if she were warning her of an oncoming motor-car. " I can see you are getting hysterical already. Now, you know that I am a friend of your mother."

" Yes," said Martha faintly.

" And you may not know that, owing to your unhappy circumstances, I am stretching a point in keeping you at the High School at a reduced rate."

" Yes, I do."

" Well, there are certain things I should like you to consider about your unfortunate position." (This must be net-ball again.)

" Has it ever occurred to you that you have certain special temptations to fight against ? "

" I suppose so." (This must mean staying in bed late in the morning.)

Making Conversation

" Has it ever occurred to you, for instance, that you have a hereditary tendency not to tell the truth ? "

Martha was struck dumb, as she had never thought of this. She now concluded Miss Spencer was trying to make her cry, as she did with a lot of the girls at music-lessons.

" It may be very difficult for you, as a result of your family history, so I want to make every allowance for you that I can. Now, your mother has written that you went to her with a tissue of lies, so foul that I cannot believe they originated in the mind of such a little girl. Is this true ? "

Martha only grinned and said, " What ?" Was Miss Spencer asking if the lies were true, or if it was true that she had told her mother the lies, which were not lies anyway ?

" Try to control yourself and concentrate ! Did you tell your mother a vile story about one of the boarders, or did you not ?"

Martha's tongue was loosened, and her face was hot and her feet cold. " Of course

Making Conversation

I told her about the things Edith did. It's perfectly true. And she knows all about you and Miss Grossmith, too."

After a minute Miss Spencer said, " Go away. I have seen enough of you for to-day."

Martha hoped she meant it. That afternoon, as she was starting for the station, she went on tip-toe past the study door, because there was always the danger that Miss Spencer would rush out and tell her she was too early. The door opened, but this time it was Miss Grossmith and not Miss Spencer. Her nose was redder than usual, and she looked as if she had been crying.

" Martha Freke," she said, " you are a disgusting little girl, and after this, no decent person will speak to you. You have a mind like a cesspool. I am ashamed of you, telling tales on your school-friends like a little sneak, and saying such things about me, when I have always been so nice to you, introducing you to my family and all when they came here, because your father was a gentleman ! "

Making Conversation

Then she stopped for breath and slapped Martha's face, which did not hurt her so much as it surprised her. Miss Grossmith flounced back into the study and banged the door, and it was too late for Martha to retaliate, even if she had felt like it, which she didn't. So she merely blew her nose, which was feeling aching and dislocated; and on her way down the High Street she examined it carefully in the mirror of Paveys' window, and was reassured to find it had not lost its shape.

That was the last time Martha went to the High School. Until the end of the term she did lessons with the Congregationalist minister's eldest daughter, who was very nice, but irreverent, because she did not give Matthew, Mark, Luke and John the title of Saint.

"I hate Dissent," said Mrs. Freke; "it is a curse to the parish. I am very broad in other directions, but not in that. They are always Radicals, too. But Mary Cook is a quiet well-spoken girl, and it's only for a short time."

Making Conversation

Mr. Lewis, the bank manager, used to help Martha with her sums when he came with the library-book. He was a little man with a moustache, who was very good-natured and used to smoke some of the cigarettes which waited in the drawing-room for a male visitor. He belonged to the demi-monde of Coombe, which included Mr. Austin, a solicitor who practised in Adderbury, and Dr. Brice. There was also Mr. Burnell, who had a mysterious position " on the roads," and a wife who was anxious to establish a footing with Mrs. Austin and Mrs. Brice. But they were none of them " county," which Mrs. Freke might have been, but for her well-known unfortunate circumstances. They did not mix with farmers, not even Big Farmers; and their urban organisation was symbolised by the Lending Library, to which they all subscribed. Martha was quite used to hearing conversations about farmers: " What wretched weather, but I suppose it's good for the farmers," or " What a lovely day, but I suppose the farmers are complaining." " Don't the farmers always complain, whatever happens ? " " Yes, they wouldn't be happy if they had nothing to complain about." Farmers were evidently irrational monsters.

Sometimes Mr. Lewis would say, " I fancy I should like to retire and settle down as a farmer. I have added up enough columns of figures."

" Don't you like mathematics ? " Martha would ask him priggishly, and he said he was sick of them. Her mother didn't like farmers, or country life in the winter, since being in India.

" If you work in the mud," she said, " you grow like the mud. What is the library-book like this time ? "

" I didn't care for it. There are no good books coming out now."

" I have a list of good books that Mrs. Montmorency sent me " (that was the paying-guest from Jamaica). " We have had nothing like *The Call of the Blood* or *The Guarded Flame* this year."

" Do you like Temple Thurston ? "

Making Conversation

"Do you mean Mr. or Mrs.?"

"I don't know the difference."

"How like a man."

"Didn't you think Mrs. Burnell's book went a little too far this time? The last chapter, where the man and woman were both reeling across the floor in a state of intoxication?"

"Yes," said Mr. Lewis, "I never object to the introduction of an element of spice, but I have no use for sordid realism. One gets plenty of it in real life without going out of one's way for more."

To Martha the terrors of the world seemed overpowering. Since she had become a pariah and social outcast in High School circles, she had an idea of what life was. When she went into Adderbury with her mother for shopping, she sometimes met High School girls who cut her dead, or made ferocious faces. Experience taught her to anticipate people who were going to cut her, by staring fixedly at their boots, or just behind their heads.

CHAPTER IV

NEXT term Martha went to the Close School. Fortunately it was quite near the station, and there was no fear of meeting her enemies on the way. Also, no one jumped out at her in the afternoons and told her she was starting home too early. In fact, Miss Robertson-Smyth, the headmistress, seemed hardly aware of Martha's existence. On the first day of the term she made a speech to the assembled school on " Community Spirit," a subject which raised Martha's suspicions and was too familiar. " We are all members one of another. A community is like the human body. If one member of it falls sick, or ceases to do its work, the whole suffers. The health of the whole depends on the co-operation of the parts. And this co-operation is to be obtained by sympathy and service."

" Robbie does this every term," said the

Making Conversation

little girl next Martha, as they floundered on to their knees for a collect. Then they got up and sang the hymn beginning " Lord, behold us with Thy blessing Once again assembled here," and filed out of the big gymnasium into the different classrooms. There were so many people in the school that Martha's brain reeled. She only knew that the gymnasium was as big as the Jubilee Hall at Coombe, where she had recited for jumble sales, and it was full of girls, with mistresses lining the walls. No drastic attempt was made to put the community spirit into practice, and no one told her she should plait her hair. There were not even any monitors. Some of the girls had funny accents.

The big girls in the domestic economy department cooked lunch, and it was not so bad as it had been at the High School, because it varied. You knew that if the meat was hard and black one day it would be soft and red the next, until the day that it was merely brown; and after that they would start on rabbits for a bit.

Making Conversation

The first unpleasantness was when Martha hadn't an overall for chemistry. "Haven't you ever done any science?" asked Miss Jones.

"No, we only did nature study."

"I see."

"And I read ' The World About Us ' in the *Children's Encyclopædia*."

Mary Street was set to help her with the experiment.

"Haven't you ever done litmuses?" she asked Martha.

"What is a lit-mouse?"

"Oh, it turns blue and red, it's topping!"

But Martha was unmoved. Then history was disappointing, because she had only done the Wars of the Roses, and knew them very well; it was a pity they didn't do them here. And the mademoiselle seemed to suffer acutely when Martha spoke French. But the Shakespeare lessons were lovely, and so was Latin translation, and French translation when you didn't have to read the French aloud.

Making Conversation

Life divided itself into term and holidays as a matter of course. It was always " Lord behold us with Thy blessing," or " Lord, dismiss us with Thy blessing " ; and it was impossible to believe that, for people who had left school, life was not divided up in this manner, but stretched before them in a featureless expanse. " It is only the division of time into days and hours and years that makes life tolerable," said Cecil Weber, one of the vicar's pupils, one evening ; and Martha agreed eagerly. Another time she came down in an orange hair-ribbon, and Cecil said that someone said that orange velvet was the only thing that reconciled one with life ; and she agreed with that, too. The war in Europe left her as unmoved as did the wonders of modern science. They were among the things that she took for granted.

" Only abnormality is amusing. Don't you agree with me, dear Mrs. Freke ? " asked Cecil. He was a charming boy of American extraction, but with hardly a trace of an American accent, and Mrs.

Making Conversation

Freke was very fond of him. She smiled enigmatically, and said that it depended.

"It is the unique sensation that counts," he went on. "One should never repeat a sensation. That is my credo."

"Yes, there I quite agree with you," said Mrs. Freke with deep conviction, and Martha wondered what she meant. It must have some reference to the past, "when I was with your father in India," when all sorts of exciting things had happened. "If there is one thing I won't stand," said Mrs. Freke, "it is being bored. Now be quiet, here's Miss Pilkington."

Cecil was older than most of the vicar's pupils; though he was very good at French and German and Italian, it seemed that he found a difficulty in getting into Oxford. He had a large head, of straight blond hair, which he held slightly on one side; blue eyes, with long eyelashes which were beautiful at a distance, but inclined to be sticky and matted; and a short nose. Miss Pilkington disliked him, although he was polite to her. Once, when she had been

Making Conversation

singing "To Julia," he said, "Pornography! Literally pornography!"

"Nonsense!" said Mrs. Freke. "It is one of the prettiest songs I know, about little elves and glow-worms."

"Pornography," he said again.

Martha looked up the word in the encyclopædia at school, which advised her to look up another word in the same " P " volume, "Prostitution." The page on which she found it was almost black from finger-marks; but the article was just legible, and she never afterwards made inapposite conversation on that and kindred subjects.

"Don't you think it is unwise," asked Miss Pilkington, "to let Martha see so much of Mr. Pyggott's young men?"

"Oh, not at all," said Mrs. Freke. "She isn't precocious in *that* way, although she is with her lessons."

"Of course not, but one has to think of the future. There is that young Weber, for instance."

Making Conversation

"A nicer boy never stepped!" said Mrs. Freke.

"I know he is a novelty to you, but when I was abroad I got quite accustomed to that type of—what shall I say?—over-*raffiné* young man. I remember one in the hotel in St. Moritz who was quite intolerable. When he walked across the lounge he used to undulate his whole body, and my brothers said he wore a pearl necklace under his sweater, though I'm sure I don't know how they could know that. I suppose it was just a joke, but you know what I mean."

"I don't know about your friend, but I know I could send Martha to the end of the world with Cecil, without fear of any harm."

"Exactly, but that is not the point!"

"Then what is the point?"

"The point is, that *nice men don't like them*."

There were no nice men left now, as they had all gone to the war. In Adderbury there were some soldiers, who used to shout

Making Conversation

humorous remarks after schoolgirls. When Martha wore her rabbit-skin gloves they called " Puss, puss ! Pretty pussy ! " and she just cut them dead, as she did her old enemies, and the Liberal Nonconformists during an election. In Coombe, one belonged to the Primrose League as one did to the Lending Library. But on the subject of rude soldiers, Martha's vanity was wounded when Margaret Hodges asked her to spend a Saturday afternoon in Adderbury, and go for a walk, " because mother won't let me go for walks with Audrey, because her eyes are too attractive." Evidently Martha's eyes had not grown.

One consolation about the war was that Miss Spencer had become a W.A.A.C. and shut up the school. " Poor Gloria ! " said Cecil. " I hope she gets a separation allowance." Occasionally the Close School helped to make paper flags for flag-days, and were let off their preparation ; but it was monotonous work, cutting up strips of red, white, blue, black, yellow and green paper for all the Allies. Mrs. Hodges had

Making Conversation

a canteen for the soldiers, and Margaret's friends used to help her. Martha went just once, and found it reminded her of the High School. Mrs. Hodges was a brisk, bright lady who was always very busy.

"Take off your coat, child," she said. But when Martha did, she said, "I think you had better put it on again, as your blouse is so transparent."

Martha blushed as she became conscious of a clean white muslin shirt-waist, with a starched embroidered camisole beneath it, which in fact entirely concealed the lines of her chest. From that day she had a horror of developing a bust like that of Mrs. Hodges, and used to rush to the mirror in the morning to see if one had grown during the night.

"You see, all the men are Tommies," continued Mrs. Hodges. "It isn't as if they were officers."

Martha was very hot in her coat, as she ran several dozen times from the kitchen to the tea-room, with trays of bread and margarine and jam, and tea mixed with

Making Conversation

milk. The soldiers said, "Thank you, miss," politely, but without enthusiasm. Once Mrs. Hodges called down the stairs: "I want a *nice* cup of cocoa, please, for a *slightly* coloured sergeant." Martha mixed it feverishly to a colour which should match the sergeant. How the colour-bar cropped up in everything.

After tea they had a song, and the helpers joined in the choruses; but Martha could not have brought herself to sing "It's a long, long trail," even if she had known it. She made a half-hearted attempt to move her lips in sympathy, partly out of politeness to the soldiers, and partly from fear of Mrs. Hodges; and on the way back, in Mr. Humphrey's waggonette, she recited to herself as much as she could remember of the *Hundred Best French Poems* and the *Selections from Horace* which they were doing at school.

It was about this time, which was early in the year 1916, that Martha became a pacificist, or, as it was incorrectly called, a "pacifist."

Making Conversation

"I do think," said Miss Pilkington one evening, "that Mr. Pyggott gives his enemies a handle. I have not heard him preach a single rousing sermon on the war."

"I should stand up for the vicar, no matter what he did," said Mrs. Freke.

Martha was being prepared for confirmation and feeling religious, so she said nothing.

"And it certainly looks suspicious," said Miss Pilkington, "that he has so many young men at the Vicarage."

"Nonsense," said Mrs. Freke, "they're all under age, or neutrals."

"And two of them with German names, Weber and Ludwig. You can't be too careful in these days. By the way, did you read that very interesting letter of the Bishop of Woollington to the *Church Times*? It explains the distinction between the duty of the State and that of the individual, and between the State in time of war and the State in time of peace. Now, a State is not the same thing as an individual." Mrs. Freke was bored. "And war is not the

Making Conversation

same as peace," went on Miss Pilkington. " So he proves, by different steps in his argument, that it may be the duty of the individual to be peaceful, but of the State to be at war ; and in that case the individual has to be at war, and at the same time—— Shall I read it to you ? "

" I'm afraid I must go and write some letters. Martha can read it aloud later on."

Martha knew she would not have to, and realised that she was beginning to regard her mother more critically than in former years. Mrs. Freke's dislike of theory was remarkable : " I don't mind what people do, as long as they do *something*," " I hate being bored," " I admire courage," " Everyone has a right to think and act as they please." Then there were the things that other people said about her, that she was such a wonderful woman, such an attractive woman, and that Martha would never be so attractive as her mother. She was dark, with flashing eyes and a large bust, and she wore her evening dresses voluptuously low in front in the Edwardian

Making Conversation

fashion. Martha had no idea how old she was.

"Darling Mrs. Freke," said Cecil Weber, when the three of them were together, " you have arrived at the most perfect age for a woman. You have got beyond the stage when they're intolerable, and Martha hasn't yet arrived at it."

They often had another visitor from the Vicarage now, called Harry Ludwig. He was not a pupil of the vicar's, but a friend, and he was writing a book. Martha found him very impressive and even nicer than Cecil; he had regular waves of blond hair, large grey eyes, a hooked nose and a large mouth. Though he was small, he had beautiful hands and feet.

" The only thing that exercises me about this war," said Cecil one evening, " is whether it will produce anything beautiful. If it does, it will have been worth while. That is the only criterion."

Miss Pilkington went to bed.

" Of course it won't," said Harry ; " it is merely retarding every movement that

Making Conversation

has been started towards making the world decently habitable. We are going back to barbarism."

"Barbarism," said Cecil, "can be very beautiful. What do you think, Martha?"

It was difficult to disagree, and she blushed violently, but had to take Harry's side. "I agree with Mr. Ludwig," she said. "Mrs. Hodges hasn't been getting any more beautiful lately."

Harry said he had to go back to work.

"Let us hope," said Cecil rather insultingly, "that your book is the moment of beauty I am waiting for."

"Is it poetry or a novel?" asked Martha.

"It's neither," he answered. "It is a general bibliography of Trade Unionism in the Transport Industry."

She did not blench, and from that moment she was a Guild Socialist. It was funny to think, as she lay in bed that night, that a short time ago she had been a Conservative, and now, without any external change, she was a Socialist. There was nothing she could do about it till the

Making Conversation

next election. She looked forward to the evenings when people came in from the Vicarage, when she put on a blue silk dress with a lace collar and cuffs. Harry taught her the initials of all the important movements.

" What's I.L.P. ? "

" Independent Labour Party."

" Right. U.D.C. ? "

" Urban District Council."

" Wrong. Union of Democratic Control. N.G.L. ? "

" National Guilds League."

" U.S.F. ? "

" University Socialist Federation."

" N.C.F. ? "

" No Conscription Fellowship."

" N.C.C. ? "

" National Council against Conscription."

" When you know these really well," he said, " I will teach you the hard ones, the N.U.S.S.C.B.B. and the A.C.U.I.S.C.W.G.B.I."

" Oh, *do* tell me what those are ! "

Making Conversation

" Those are the National Union of Ships' Stewards, Cooks, Butchers and Bakers, and the Amalgamated Coal-porters Union of Inland and Seaborne Coal Workers of Great Britain and Ireland."

" Oh dear ! "

" Do you know the difference between a docker and a stevedore ? "

" No."

" I'm not sure that I do either."

CHAPTER V

THE trouble started with Mrs. Hodges, when she met Mrs. Freke in Paveys' shop in Adderbury one morning, and Mrs. Freke asked her to come in to tea. Mrs. Hodges banged her big, unrolled umbrella on the counter and said, " Tea ! My good woman, do you think I have time for tea ? Here is the whole world at war, and you ask me to tea ! "

Mrs. Freke said she was sorry, and Mrs. Hodges said well she might be. " And you people at Coombe, with that vicar of yours, you'll find yourselves in a tight corner one day. Harbouring German spies, that's what it is ! "

" Nonsense," said Mrs. Freke.

" Well, what about that fellow Weber ? "

" He's an American."

" American, my hat ! He is accepting English hospitality. Where are his guts, that's what I should like to know ? "

Making Conversation

Mrs. Freke said she had never asked him. Soon afterwards came the mysterious affair of the R.S.P.C.A., which was not a trades union, but the Royal Society for the Prevention of Cruelty to Animals. The Frekes had an old donkey called Katy, which Martha had ridden when she was small. Katy's teeth were very bad, and she ate less and less, and soon she would have to be shot. Mrs. Freke did not think of Katy when Ellen came in one morning and said there was a gentleman at the door saying he was an inspector. The police, she thought, the Defence of the Realm Act, Ludwig, the No Conscription Fellowship ! When they came to fetch her poor husband there had been two of them, but perhaps it was different with political crimes. She was a brave woman, and patted her hair at the mirror before she went into the drawing-room. There was a man there, but he had taken his hat off.

" Mrs. Freke ? " he asked, and she said, " Yes."

" I am here," he said, " on behalf of the

Making Conversation

Royal Society for the Prevention of Cruelty to Animals. We have received information at headquarters that you are treating an animal in a manner which is, er, tantamount to cruelty; and I have come to investigate."

She breathed again, and wanted to laugh, but bewilderment followed. Sambo the cat at this moment rubbed himself, purring, against the inspector's leg.

" An animal ? "

" Yes, an ass."

" Oh, the poor old donkey ! I assure you——"

She led him to the orchard, and on the way they passed another fat cat and numbers of well-fed chickens.

" I was given to understand," he said, " that the ass was starved."

After an examination of Katy he apologised and explained that malicious communications were often received.

" I'm sure it was Mrs. Hodges," said Mrs. Freke that evening.

" Are you sure he wasn't a police-spy ? " asked Ludwig.

Making Conversation

" What nonsense ! What would a police-spy want in our orchard ? Poor old Katy ! She enjoys her life. I don't believe in taking the life of anything that enjoys it."

" You are a true hedonist," said Cecil.

" I wonder," said Harry, " if that's a tenable theory for the N.C.F. I might work it into a pamphlet."

The next day he organised a tea-party in Adderbury for a mysterious purpose. He invited the vicar and Cecil and Mrs. Freke and Martha to tea in Stephens' tea-rooms, where they had some nasty war-time cakes which tasted of sawdust and were coloured pink with cochineal. There was a girl at a piano, and a man with a squeaky violin, and they played " Indian Love-lyrics " and " I'll sing thee songs of Araby." Harry said the man at the next table might be a police-spy. Afterwards they went to a room over a shop in Abbey Street, and burned a lot of papers in the fire-grate. They were pamphlets headed " Peace, Perfect Peace " and " To Sweethearts and Wives " ; and there were some

Making Conversation

in verse about English and French and German and Russian peasants, who said in the chorus:

> "*I cannot tell, but this I know,
> I fought because they told me so.*"

After a bit, Harry said they must carry the rest away. The men stuffed some into their pockets, and Martha asked if she might be allowed to hide some in her underclothes. She was wearing a sensible pair of navy-blue gym knickers, with elastic at the knee. But unfortunately, she stuffed them too tight, and as they were walking down the High Street, the elastic gave way, and the pamphlets were blown along the pavement. A kind old gentleman helped her to collect them. He must have been fairly blind, because he said, "Now, what's this? Not peace propaganda, I hope?" Which was exactly what they were.

The next excitement was Harry's tribunal, in Adderbury Town Hall. It was in a dark room with ugly panelling and bad stained-glass windows. The chairman of

Making Conversation

the bench was the mayor, Sir Robert Budgett, who was very old, with a white beard; and there were a lot of other shopkeepers. The sharp little man in an officer's uniform, who asked Harry questions, was the military representative, Captain Huggins. He was really a lawyer in disguise. "Now, Mr. Ludwig," he said, "what would you do, if you were walking along the street, and you met a mad dog?"

"I should run away," said Harry.

"Wouldn't you use force?"

"Certainly not!" And everybody laughed.

"Germany," said the military representative, "is the mad dog of Europe. Come now, Mr. Ludwig, what does the Bible say? Doesn't it say an eye for an eye, and a tooth for a tooth?"

"No, it doesn't," said Harry with a broad smile.

"'No, it doesn't'? Well, if I had a Bible, I could find it for you."

"If it is a question of theology," said Harry, "you had better ask my friend, the

Making Conversation

Vicar of Coombe, who is here to give evidence."

" Very well, now. What would have happened if Belgium had not had an army?"

" Belgium would have been much safer without an army."

A pause, while the shopkeepers looked puzzled.

" What about Luxembourg?" asked Captain Huggins triumphantly.

" Before I answer that question," said Harry, " I should like to know exactly what *did* happen in Luxembourg."

The tribunal then called Mr. Pyggott, who said he had known Harry a long time, and could testify to his character, and that he was engaged in research work of national importance. So they adjourned his case for six months, and went on with some Christadelphians, whom they polished off very soon.

Mrs. Freke and Martha took Harry out to tea in triumph, and Mrs. Freke said she didn't care twopence for his principles, but she did like courage. It was a severe

Making Conversation

shock to them when they heard, two days later, that he had been arrested for disseminating seditious literature under the Defence of the Realm Act, and was in Adderbury County Gaol. Martha wept floods of tears at the idea of Harry's hair being cropped close, and Harry in broad arrows, picking oakum.

"No, dear," said her mother, "they won't give him hard labour until after they've tried him. He's only on remand."

Martha was sure that nothing but the collapse of her elastic was responsible, and she had never been so unhappy in her life. The gaol was a hideous neo-Gothic building near the station, which she saw every day on her way to school, and it was there that Harry was pacing his cell, like a caged animal. Margaret Hodges wouldn't speak to her in the lunch-hour, but that was a consolation, to suffer something for him. Her sense of sin was evident at her confirmation-classes, and perhaps the vicar told Harry about it, when he was allowed to visit him. Anyway, beyond all expectation,

Making Conversation

she got a letter, on prison blue note-paper, in an official envelope of a different colour, saying " On His Majesty's Service." She felt sardonic about the service His Majesty was doing her. At the top of the page she was told " in replying to this letter please write on the envelope: Number 788, Name, H. Ludwig, Prison, Adderbury." He said:

" DEAR MARTHA,—There is really remarkably little to record: prison does not materially increase one's stock of anecdotes. There is absolutely nothing wrong with prison, except the general principle of not being free; but I am longing to get out for the next coffee-party at Hillview. I must apologise for my calligraphy (or should I say cacography?), which is due to the fact that His Majesty is in possession of my fountain-pen. But I hope he will be kind enough to let you and your mother come to see me one day soon. Love to you all from

" HARRY."

Making Conversation

Martha slept with this under her pillow. It was disappointing in some ways, but evidently he could not describe his tortures in detail, or the letter would have been suppressed. Two days later, she and her mother went to visit the prison.

A little door opened in the big Gothic gateway, and they were shown into a lodge. A fat man telephoned, " Two young ladies to see Number 788," and they were both flattered at being thought to be contemporaries. They went across a courtyard into a room with a fireplace, a long table covered with green baize, and some chairs. There was a clock ticking on the mantelpiece. They sat at one side of the table, and Martha had a dentist-feeling at the thought of Harry's cropped head. But he came in, between two warders, in his ordinary clothes and with his usual curls, and said, " Hullo ! " cheerfully.

He asked her about school and Margaret Hodges, and thanked Mrs. Freke for a cake. They all said several times that they were very well, and Harry asked them to

Making Conversation

thank the vicar for some books. He said the prison library was rather limited; it had too many copies of a book called *It Cometh Up as a Flower*. They seemed to have been there no time when the warder said, " Time's up ! " and took Harry out. He was not allowed to shake hands. That must have been for fear they would pass him files, thought Martha, to cut his chains. She thought afterwards of many things she meant to ask him—for instance, if he had spiders in his cell like Robert Bruce. He could not have been so cheerful as he seemed ; but at least he did not blame her for his incarceration.

The next excitement was the trial. There were a lot of people from London, who were talking in initials, but gave Martha no chance of joining in the conversation. They mostly wore eye-glasses and terrible clothes, but she was prepared to put up with that, if they would only treat her properly. She overheard such expressions as alternative service, court martial, civil prison, breaking stones in Aberdeenshire,

Making Conversation

mine-sweeping, ambulance-units, clause 2, sub-section 3. She and her mother and Cecil had a good seat in the gallery. The vicar was underneath in a kind of pew near Harry, with a man from London; and it was a dark, panelled room again, and there were more shopkeepers in a row. When the judge came in, they got up as if it were church. Martha wanted to sit still, to show her contempt for the proceedings, but was pulled up by her mother. She was furious when Harry pleaded " Not guilty," as he ought to have been proud of what he had done. But her mother said everyone always pleaded " Not guilty," and then they could appeal against their sentences afterwards.

The evidence was quite short, and they read out some of the pamphlets. A lawyer got up and made a speech about King and country, and German gold, and aliens and spies, and dangers to our State, which was very stupid. But Harry's lawyer was rather bad, too, and Martha thought he didn't go far enough. He insisted on talking about

Making Conversation

Harry's brother at the " Front," and their poor old father and mother. When the judge began to sum up, he was kind and nice, though evidently old and stupid. He said Harry was very young and thoughtless, and no danger to " our State," and Martha was sure he would let him off. But then he began, " On the other hand," and contradicted all he had said before. The shopkeepers went out for a little while ; and when they came back, Harry was sentenced to two months in the Second Division.

All his friends were whispering about " appeals," and it seemed he would be let out again while his appeal was pending. He came out of the court quite free, and Martha nearly fainted from excitement while they waited for him downstairs. Then his friends from London surrounded him and said, " What about lunch ? "

Of course, they would invite her too. Harry came up and shook her hand. " Good-bye, Martha," he said ; " I'm afraid I won't see you again for a bit. I'm going up to London until my appeal."

Making Conversation

She never saw him again.

Miss Pilkington left Hillview. One day after tea, Martha was in the drawing-room with Mrs. Freke, doing her lessons. She had decided to devote her talents to the Socialist Movement, and as she did her algebra homework, she thought of being a statistician. One day when she had become famous, she would meet Harry in a research department, and possibly put him right on some minute point. She would never marry him ; but she might live with him for a time, on a basis of strict equality.

The door burst open ; Cecil ran in, and kissed Mrs. Freke reverently on the forehead.

" May I come and live here always ? " he asked. " May I have my name on a little card on the door ? "

" Of course, dear. What has happened ? "

" The poor vicar ! Those brutes have got him ! "

" Who ? "

" The police."

" What for ? "

Making Conversation

" They left a summons on him. For harbouring an unregistered alien ; doesn't it sound too hideous ? Under the Defence of the Realm Act. There was a detective, a great, coarse man with big boots, who asked him the most *obscene* questions, I really couldn't tell you."

" A plain-clothes man," said Mrs. Freke. In the poor major's case there had been two of them. (" Two gentlemen to see you in the hall, sir.")

" It seems they have been observing us," said Cecil, " in the most intimate phases of our daily lives ! Then the policeman came with the summons, and he has to go to the court to-morrow. Look ! You must register me as an alien at once, and I have brought you this beautiful book from the Omega Workshop. The paper is handmade. What colour ink shall we use ? "

Mr. Pyggott was fined 10*s*. 6*d*. for his offence against the realm ; but that was not the worst. People began to throw stones at the Vicarage windows, and to write rude remarks on his gate. Then he went away,

Making Conversation

and the bishop sent someone else in his place, a red-faced man with a wife and six children. The Frekes stopped going to church, and Martha was never confirmed, so she ceased to be an Anglican, except when filling in forms. After the Easter-week Rebellion in Ireland, she thought of becoming a Catholic.

"I hate the Irish!" said Margaret Hodges.

"I adore them!" said Martha, who knew nothing about them, but found constant pleasure in disagreeing with Margaret. It was usually much more pleasant to agree with people.

"Mummy hates them," said Margaret. "She used to have a very good time staying in Ireland, but now she says she'll never forgive them."

Martha thought the Irish must have had some sense, to get rid of Mrs. Hodges. "Oh, why?" she asked.

"Because they've stabbed us in the back."

"Who are you, anyway?"

Making Conversation

" Us, the British, of course ! "

" And a very good thing, too ! " said Martha vaguely.

Margaret refused to speak to her any more, and ran across the playground, stamping her feet in soft gym shoes on the asphalt pavement, with a violence which must have hurt her.

" Bertrand Russell," explained Martha to the other girls who were there, " says it would be a pity if either side won the war, and it would be much better if it stopped before anyone found out which it was."

But it was soon after this that she received another severe blow. Cecil went to London and met Harry, who sent his love.

" He said something else about you, Martha," said Cecil, with a malevolent glint in his eye, and an insincere smile. " Only I don't know if I ought to tell you."

" Oh, do ! "

" I don't agree with him myself. But he said, ' Is she really at all clever ? Because she always seems to agree with everything one says.' "

CHAPTER VI

Life was dull without Mr. Pyggott's pupils; but Martha took an increasing interest in literature, and less in statistics. Cecil was still there, and sometimes said, " Martha, shall we read a little Horace ? " But he had a dishonest habit of finding a book with a crib, and giving her the text by itself. He told her there were poems of Catullus she wasn't allowed to read at school ; but it was obvious that if she couldn't understand them, he couldn't either. At this time she agreed with Byron that poetry should be simple and sensuous, and was on principle a sensationalist rather than an intellectual. But as she didn't do anything but read books, no one noticed the difference. She wrote an essay on Keats, about loading every rift with ore, and inevitably introduced the remark about beauty being truth, and truth beauty.

" It's a pity you don't know Italian,"

Making Conversation

said Cecil, " or you could read D'Annunzio. Except that he is almost more exquisite in translation."

At school they were " doing " the French Romantic Movement, and she had a passion for the plays of Victor Hugo. The romantic hero seemed always to be illegitimate, and she wondered if Cecil might be that, as he was melancholy and sufficiently handsome, except that his head was large in proportion to his body. He never spoke of his family, and the allowance which arrived from America somewhat irregularly might be from an illegitimate father. Then there were poems about consumptives walking in decaying woods in the autumn ; and she wondered if she had a tendency to consumption herself, which she had not.

In the winter of 1916, Mrs. Freke heard from her Uncle Randolph, who had been in the Diplomatic Service. After an honourable and undistinguished career, he had retired to Wimbledon, and was now on a committee for helping Serbian refugees.

Making Conversation

He suggested sending two of these to his niece as boarders, at a reduced rate. " After my long experience as second in command to Sir Philip Wimple at Belgrade, I can give you the key-note to the racial psychology of the southern Slav : he can be led, but never driven. If you keep this in mind, I see no reason why the arrangement should not be very satisfactory ; and I could not find you a nicer pair of boys than Dragoljub Popovitch and Milenko Jovanovitch."

" I'm afraid they will be very dreadfully crude," said Cecil.

" Won't they be very militarist ? " asked Martha.

When they arrived at Adderbury station, Dragoljub and Milenko were looking cold, in spite of the sensible clothes and brown mufflers provided by Uncle Randolph's committee. They were also tongue-tied because they were tired ; and they thought that definite and indefinite articles were unnecessary in a language. Both were tall and swarthy, and as they thawed by the drawing-room fire, it became evident that they

Making Conversation

were dreams of beauty. They ate hot cakes hungrily, but did not forget their manners.

" Are you fond of music ? " asked Mrs. Freke.

" Oh, yes ! We like *very* much ! "

Their vowel sounds were odd, but their voices musical, and they spoke English better than the Japanese.

" In our country, we have very fine national music and dances. We shall show you," said Dragoljub.

Martha, as an internationalist, felt superior.

" You have also in England national dances," he went on.

" Oh, no," she said ; " only some very stupid and noisy things that are quite bogus."

" What is bogus ? "

" I mean, not genuine. And folky. Only danced by peasants."

" In Serbia," said Dragoljub, " everyone is peasant."

As a Socialist, Martha had been caught out, and she looked uncomfortable.

Making Conversation

" In music of nation," he went on, " and dances of nation, is soul of nation."

Cecil smiled an irritating smile. " It seems rather pointless," he said, " to fight a lot of wars about a particular method of kicking one's legs, don't you think ? "

Martha defended Dragoljub. " I think it's all right," she said, " for small nations to be patriotic. It's only when big ones are, like the English, that they're so awful."

Dragoljub missed the point. " Dancing is symbol," he said. " When foreigners invade country, they suppress old national customs. In our country, we have suffered. We stand between East and West. We are defenders of Europe."

Mrs. Freke and Martha and Cecil were all vague about the history of Eastern Europe. " Have you both fought yourselves ? " asked Mrs. Freke.

" Oh, yes," said Dragoljub and Milenko.

" My husband," she said, " was in British Army." She was infected by their habit of omitting the article.

Making Conversation

"We fought," said Dragoljub, "in Serbian Army in retreat."

She wasn't sure what retreat that was, but said it must have been terrible.

"Oh, yes, it was terrible. Very cold in mountains, very much snow. Many people are frozen. But in Corfu was worse. In Corfu, many soldiers eat for first time, eat too quickly bad food, many thousands die. We throw bodies into sea. Smell was terrible."

He turned a flashing eye on her, and tossed a lock of jet-black hair off his forehead. Everyone found the conversation embarrassing.

"Terrible!" repeated Mrs. Freke. "And by the way, as we are on the subject of food, is there anything you can't eat?"

"Oh, yes, in Corfu one must be very careful, especially in hot weather."

"I mean *here*, is there anything you do not eat, must not eat?"

He bared some excellent teeth in a smile. "Oh, no! I beg your pardon! We

Making Conversation

like very much everything. Sometimes we must fast for our religion. But then we eat nothing."

" Oh, yes, of course, you are Catholics."

" Of course not, mamma ; they're Greek Orthodoxes," said Martha breathlessly. " You know that perfectly well."

" Ort-o-dox," said Dragoljub, " not Roman Catholic. But Anglican Church is so kind to us. It is practically same thing. You are Anglican ? "

" Yes," said Mrs. Freke, " Church of England."

This hypocrisy infuriated Martha, who knew her mother had not been to church for months, and that she never knelt down to say her prayers.

" Martha and I are free-thinkers," announced Cecil with a smile.

Milenko showed signs of animation for the first time, and sat up with a jump.

" Oh, no," said Dragoljub, " that is impossible ! " He stared at her in amazement, and she just managed to return his stare. His eyes were set far apart under a

Making Conversation

wide forehead ; he had a straight nose with curling nostrils ; and full lips which, against his dark skin, seemed to have a bluish tinge, but that might have been the cold. Milenko had brown hair, and long, deep-set grey eyes; and he was not quite so big.

" Why is it impossible ? " asked Martha with a superior smile.

" Oh, it is quite impossible ! Such a young girl, and so nice and kind ! "

" I expect you would like to see your rooms," said Mrs. Freke, and took the exiles upstairs.

" A little crude," said Cecil, when the door was shut.

" Yes, but they're rather sweet," said Martha, " if only they wouldn't talk about atrocities."

The next day, which was Sunday, Dragoljub and Milenko revealed that they were theological students. Martha was excited to learn that they knew liturgical Greek ; but she did not make much headway with a conversation about the Greek drama. They

Making Conversation

did not seem to recognise her pronunciation of any classical names; and this was disappointing, as they were doing the *Alcestis* at school. Mrs. Freke took the two young men to church, while Martha and Cecil stayed at home by the fire. The others came back in high spirits, too hot and hearty after their walk, and were very hungry for lunch.

" When you go home," asked Martha, " will you both be priests ? "

" Oh, yes, perhaps, if we pass examinations," said Dragoljub.

" Were you a student before you were in the army ? "

" Yes, I was student. I was also schoolmaster."

" Really, how interesting ! Did you like it ? "

" Oh, yes, it was in country. Children were very nice, very naughty. I liked them very much. One day, I hear inspector is coming. Children still very naughty, so I join band of *komitadji* instead."

" A band of what ? "

Making Conversation

"*Komitadji.* I don't think you have that in England. People travel all over country, everywhere."

"I don't know," said Martha. "Perhaps it's something like the W.E.A.; I mean the Workers' Educational Association, people who go round the country lecturing."

She looked them up later in the encyclopædia, which said they were a type of brigand.

Cecil offered to give English lessons to Dragoljub and Milenko, and Mrs. Freke said he was very kind.

"Don't say that!" he implored her. "That is the cruellest thing you could say to me!"

"Then why are you doing it if you are not kind?"

"Because they would be less attractive," he said, "if they spoke better English. And then I should not be so jealous of them."

So they started an advanced course of reading with Pater on *The Renaissance*; and his pupils thought him very kind, and the

Making Conversation

book very difficult. They asked him and Mrs. Freke and Martha to call them Dragan and Misha. And on Christmas Day, they sent to Martha cards inscribed: Συγχαίρω σοί το νεὸν ἔτος ὅ ἔρχεται, χρήζω ὑπερπολλας τὰς εὐδαιμονίας καὶ τόν πολὺν βίον, τῇ μῆτρι σοῦ πέμπω ἀστείας εὔνοιας.

Dragan and Misha wore ready-made dark grey suits provided by something called " the Fund," but they no longer wore the khaki scarves with which they had arrived. Martha hated khaki anyway, and the scarves looked like British Army misfits; so she was delighted when Mrs. Freke gave them bright Fair Isle scarves for Christmas.

" Oh, they are beautiful!" said Dragan.

" We have also in Serbia," said Misha, " *des broderies comme ça.*"

" Yes, I remember," said Mrs. Freke, " during the Balkan wars, there was quite a fashion for embroideries." Why did they always look annoyed when someone remembered something about the Balkans? " I remember," she went on, " some delicious Bulgarian embroideries."

Making Conversation

Misha developed a deep vertical wrinkle between his narrow grey eyes. "Bulgarians!" he said. "*Ce n'est pas la même chose.*"

"Bulgarians," said Dragan, "are Huns of the Near East. I could tell you——"

"Never mind, dear," said Mrs. Freke. "Don't let us think of things like that on Christmas Day."

They wore the scarves with an air, as they walked up and down the New Road, a straight road over the moors, which had been there as long as Martha could remember, and which she connected with compulsory exercise. She wore a navy-blue overcoat over her usual white shirt-blouse and blue serge skirt; and on Sundays she wore a newer and better navy-blue coat and skirt. As the young men were much taller than she was, she got very hot, and panted, in her efforts to keep up with them; but she managed to talk all the same, and they could not keep up with her conversation. "It's so good for her," said her mother to Cecil, "going for walks and talking more."

Making Conversation

The Hodges family grew more disapproving, even though the Serbs were gallant allies. " Well, how are your slackers and shirkers ? " said Mrs. Hodges to Mrs. Freke, at the annual meeting of the Primrose League.

" I don't know whom you are referring to," said Mrs. Freke. If she had not been on her dignity, she would have said " who " instead of " whom."

" Herr Weber, for instance," said Mrs. Hodges, pronouncing it in a super-German accent, " Hair Vay-ber," whereas he was usually called " Webber."

" Nonsense," said Mrs. Freke, which was what she always said when she was attacked. " He's very busy teaching the Serbs."

" Teaching them ! And what is he teaching them, I should like to know ? " She didn't wait for an answer. " Treason !" —she went on—" Treason ! " and then turned her back.

It would have been difficult to undermine the patriotism of Dragan and Misha.

Making Conversation

Dragan told Martha how his pupils happened to be unprepared for the visit of the school-inspector. " I teach them to act plays from Serbian history, Battle of Kossovo, Milosh Obrenovitch, Kralievitch Marko, many national heroes. They fight quite a lot." She said it was a pity to foster the natural militarist impulses of children; and she preferred discussing literary criticism.

" I don't know what you feel about cricitism," she said one day on the New Road. " Of course, Anatole France says the critic only has to read books, and describe his adventures afterwards. But Matthew Arnold thinks it is much more complicated than that. He says that art stands in the same relation to life as criticism does to art. I mean that criticism has to art the same relation that art has to life, and that is very important, obviously, isn't it ? "

" Oh, *yes* ! " they both said enthusiastically.

" You ought to read Arnold's essays on

Making Conversation

criticism. There are standards in criticism which have to be kept up. And you ought to read the *Nation* and the *New Statesman* and the *Times Literary Supplement*. I must get mamma to take them regularly." She stopped for breath.

"Critics are terrible," said Dragan, "oh, terrible!"

"Oh, why?" asked Martha, and then went on, "Yes, I know some of them are. Some people said it was critics who killed Keats. The poet, you know, who wrote that beautiful 'Ode to a Nightingale' I read you. And that's why Shelley wrote 'Adonais.' But he would have died, anyway; he had consumption. You know, tuberculosis, phthisis. And they are very necessary; I mean critics."

"They are parasites," said Dragan, "insects, Germans."

Martha had hardly ever seen a German; and as a result of growing up during the Great War, she thought they must be the nicest people in the world. So this fell flat.

Making Conversation

Misha explained, " He is poet."

" Oh, is he really ? How thrilling ! Has he ever published any poems ? "

" Yes, he published, in review in Beograd."

" Well, of course, a real creative artist is better than critics. But really good critics create something themselves. You like Pater, don't you ? "

" Oh, yes," they said, " we like very much."

That night in bed, Martha thought of Dragan in his new character of poet. He was also a theological student, and had been a type of brigand, and was an unthinking militarist. She was not ignorant enough to imagine that Orthodox priests were celibate, and wondered what it would be like to be married to him in Serbia. It would be impossible for herself to be a parson's wife, and help in the parish. If all the priests were forced to marry, there must be a dull type of girl reared for the purpose. That was a pity, as he was very handsome. But Orthodox priests were

Making Conversation

rather exciting and exotic, and they had a beautiful ritual, and eikons in the churches. She might make a collection of eikons. Or if Dragan had a great success as a poet, he might give up the Church, and be a man of letters. They might start a literary magazine in Beograd after the war. She would write the book-reviews, and they would have a salon of writers and painters and sculptors. Mestrovitch was a Serbian. Women in those countries got their clothes from Vienna. If she married, she would have to have children, which was boring. But foreign children would be more amusing than English ones; they would grow up speaking several languages, and would be a practical experiment in internationalism. The salon would be very cosmopolitan. Would the children be liable to conscription in the Serbian Army? They had a lot of wars and revolutions in those countries. How awful if Dragan himself were killed in a rising! He said many of his friends belonged to secret societies. He knew a Bosnian who was the next man to draw

Making Conversation

his lot before the man who had to assassinate the archduke at Sarajevo. She would enjoy being a revolutionary woman : disguises, secret messages, meetings in cellars, documents in code, and pretending not to recognise one's friends in the tram-car. Then she imagined her feelings as a widow. Would she commit suicide ? No, she would be brave and live for her children. She squeezed out a few tears, and went to sleep comfortably on a moist pillow.

CHAPTER VII

THE Christmas holidays came to an end, and, early next term, Mrs. Freke thought it would be nice to have a party. Martha could ask some girls from school, not including Margaret Hodges. Dragan and Misha were asked if they would like to invite anyone, but they said their friends were all far away. Mrs. Freke hated dwelling on the subject of exile, and asked if there wasn't anyone in London.

"Oh, yes," said Dragan, "we have great friend in Wimbledon. But he is monk."

"A monk? I didn't know you had them. I thought only Catholics had monks."

"Oh, yes, we have many monks. With us, all bishops are monks. Saint Sava, our patron saint, was prince and also monk."

"Well, I don't know if your friend would care to come to a party, if he's a monk."

Making Conversation

"Oh, he is so nice! He would like very much!"

"Then ask him to come down for a few days, and I will arrange it with my uncle. What does he eat? What does the monk eat?"

"Oh, thank you, thank you very much! He eats very little. He drinks cold water. And he eats very dry bread, small pieces, I forget the name."

"Unleavened bread?" asked Mrs. Freke.

"Oh, no, you eat it in England with cheese."

"Biscuits!" said Mrs. Freke and Martha simultaneously, in tones of relief.

"Yes. And perhaps a little jam."

"Well, that's simple. What is his name?"

"Velisar. Brother Velisar. In English you have the name Belisarius."

They were too polite to say it was not a common name.

"If he lives on jam and biscuits, he won't be much trouble," said Mrs. Freke to Martha and Cecil later, "but I think the cooking has been getting beyond Ellen

Making Conversation

lately. What about getting one of those Belgian refugees ? "

" Surely two refugees in one house are enough," said Cecil ; " and Serbs at least are not so terribly obvious."

" But Belgians help with the cooking in return for board and lodging, poor things," said Mrs. Freke.

So Monsieur and Madame Michiels were provided by another Fund. As they arrived at the station, a fussy fellow-passenger put her head out of the window and said, " Here are some Belgians I've been asked to deliver." Monsieur Michiels was sulky, and no wonder. He was a fat man with a beautiful complexion and golden hair and beard, and his name was Gustave. Madame was called Mathilde, and she was more polite and grateful, but inclined to tears. She had a complexion tinged with purple, a large bust, well-corseted hips, and tiny hands and feet. She wore a navy-blue costume which was shiny, but beautifully pressed and brushed, and a large black velvet hat.

Making Conversation

" Poor thing," said Martha, " If I were a refugee, I wouldn't brush my clothes. I should be only too glad of the excuse to let myself go."

" That's the last thing you would ever do," said Cecil, " let yourself go ! "

" I don't know. I sometimes think it would be nice to be a Homeric scholar or an archæologist or something, and devote my life to it, and not bother about anything else, and get lice in my hair."

" Talking of lice," he said, " do beards appeal to you ? "

" Not particularly, but Monsieur's is ever so clean. How old do you think he is ? "

Dragan and Misha were sure he was quite young, and anxious to avoid military service.

The Michiels did not contribute much to the intellectual life of Hillview, but made themselves felt on the material side. They asked for cheese at breakfast, after working through the English dishes, which are never so good as they look, and were worse than usual in 1917.

Making Conversation

"My husband, madame, he is still hungry," said Madame Michiels; but they both fell on the small piece of mature Cheddar, divided it, and swallowed the bits without enthusiasm, grunting in an incomprehensible language which must be Flemish.

"I'm afraid they must be rather common," said Mrs. Freke, "Only the lower classes in Belgium speak Flemish. And I was sure they would have a Continental breakfast. But they're very nice and clean and polite."

In the mornings, Madame appeared in a beautiful embroidered white gown, as loose as a nightdress, because she could not cook in her stays. She could not even button her tiny shoes, so Ellen did that for her, shouting in the loud voice she used for foreigners, "All right, madam, Ellen'll do ut for 'ee."

Madame used a terrible amount of butter in the cooking, and insisted on making soup for lunch every day, and two lots of "*patâtes frites*." Martha knew that

Making Conversation

could not possibly be French, and she did not talk much Belgian French to the Michiels, for fear of spoiling the purity of her accent. At least, that was a good excuse for not making conversation at all. Monsieur's range of topics was limited, and he was most fond of talking of the lady they had lived with before, who had not given them enough to eat. "*Vieille salope*," he called her; and his favourite interjections were "*Ouais!*" and "*Allons donc!*" and "*Par exemple!*" Between meals, he spent most of the time in his bedroom working out schemes for a new line of trade in horse-flesh between Bristol and Antwerp. There was nothing in it, but it was the only possible recreation for a business man under the circumstances.

"They keep that fire burning night and day, and coal the price it is," Mrs. Freke used to complain ineffectually. "They say they have central heating at home, but I can hardly believe it." As she watched Madame cook in the mornings, she heard of the comforts of their house in the

Making Conversation

suburbs of Antwerp, their brass ornaments, their linen and their little dog ; how in the afternoon one might take one's needlework to the park, and in the evening one might go with one's husband to the café.

Any reference to alcohol, and Mrs. Freke pricked up her ears. It was one of the causes of the major's downfall, and she had no taste for it herself. " Ah, but you have nice light beer abroad," she said. Just as she said " the Balkans " to the Serbs, she said " abroad " to the Belgians. But the theory about light beer went the same way as the one about Continental breakfast. " All beer is good, madame," said Madame Michiels. " You have in England very good beer, Guinness. We must have beer, madame. My husband is not well since the *bombardement*."

At any mention of the *bombardement*, Mrs. Freke gave in, whether it was a question of coal, or butter, or cheese, or celery soup, or an unaccustomed cut of beef for "*-carbonate flamande*." The beer annoyed her, as she had to get it from the

Making Conversation

Bath Arms, and she had no relations with public houses, except to call at the side door to order a waggonette. She had never been in a bar, and did not want to send Ellen, so Cecil ordered the beer. Mrs. Freke's idea of drink was a bottle of white wine at lunch, which she did not drink herself; and for dinner, in exceptional cases, claret and port, which she did not drink either; these were only for parties, and not every day. In detecting intoxication, she relied entirely on her sense of smell.

It was in connection with the Michiels that Martha discovered she was a Manichæan or Bogumil. On a Saturday morning, she was called into the kitchen to take part in a controversy on the relation of *endive* to *chicorée*; and she was sulky.

" You might put yourself out a little, dear," said her mother. " What is the use of a distinction in French in the School Certificate if you don't apply your knowledge? Couldn't you look it up in your *Petit Larousse* ? "

Making Conversation

Martha went back to the breakfast-room, where Dragan and Misha were working. (Cecil was still in bed.) " I hate housekeeping," she said ; " I think it's waste of time. I don't want to apply my knowledge to vegetables."

" You are Bogumil," said Dragan.

" What on earth is that ? "

" They are heretics we have in our country ; they think the world is a bad place."

" So do I."

" They believe only in the spirit. They say God made the spirit, Devil made the flesh. Devil made the world. They say spirit and flesh are always fighting. Sometimes they live together in villages and share everything, have no property."

" I see, they're kind of Socialists."

" They are heretics. Often, in theological seminary, we say to each other ' Bogumil.' "

" Then I think I'll say I'm a Bogumil. The world is so awful, I can't believe God made it, especially snakes and flies. Is Brother Velisar a Bogumil ? "

Making Conversation

"Oh, no, he is philosopher. He writes a thesis on the philosophy of Dostoevsky."

That started her reading translations of Russian novels; and she was interested in everything rather than the philosophy. She adored a chapter called " Lacerations " in the Brothers Karamazov, and she loved *The Idiot* and *Crime and Punishment*. This was life. She read *Anna Karenina*, and imagined how she would feel as an unfaithful wife; and there was *War and Peace* too, but she skipped a lot of that.

Brother Velisar arrived the day before the party. He wore a long black gown; a black felt hat, under which his black hair streamed down to his shoulders; and he had a black beard as well, and a pale face and piercing eyes. Martha felt an insane desire to giggle. "We *are* running to beards!" said Cecil, in a rude aside. Monsieur Michiels was clearly hostile, anti-clerical and freemasonic; and his wife, who was a suppressed Catholic, was overcome with confusion.

" I expect you would like to go and see

Making Conversation

your room, Father," said Mrs. Freke. She always called priests Father, and when she met them at any distance from Coombe, hoped they would mistake her for a Catholic. He bowed in silence, and took up a little black Gladstone bag, which was all the luggage he had. Monsieur Michiels went upstairs too, and did not come down for tea. There were loud and cheerful noises in a foreign tongue from the monk's room, which was the small one over the hall ; Misha had turned out of it, and was sleeping on the sofa in Dragan's room next door. When the three young men reappeared, they were quiet again, and Dragan said his friend must be excused for speaking bad English. The monk looked younger and nicer without a hat, and his hair was brushed straight back from a beautiful forehead. He did not drink water after all, but succeeded in bowing twice to indicate two lumps of sugar in his tea. Martha put a small bamboo table beside him, with a plate of Huntley & Palmer's cream crackers, and a dish of home-made

Making Conversation

strawberry jam. He bowed again and began to eat the jam by itself with his teaspoon. Mrs. Freke watched him in amazement, and then averted her eyes. Conversation went on as usual. After tea she called Martha into the smoking-room, and said, " Did you see his eyes ? Do you think he's mad ? "

" No, mamma, I'm sure he isn't. He's only shy, and, being a monk and all, I expect he feels strange."

" But did you see him eating up all the jam ? "

" Oh, that's nothing ! " said Martha in a superior tone. " That's a Slavonic custom, like having lemons in your tea. They do it in Russian novels. They always bring out the samovar and some preserves, especially priests."

" But I remember one of Dr. Brice's patients, when he used to take mental cases without getting them certified. It was at a Primrose League committee meeting, and no one took much notice of the poor woman, I thought she was just a paying-guest.

Making Conversation

She sat there and didn't say a word, and when she came in, she began stuffing herself with jam out of a spoon. Then I saw Mrs. Brice looking at her and looking at the doctor, and she was *quite* loony. They ought never to have had her there at all, but her family paid very well. By the way, Ellen says he has nothing in that bag but books, no underclothes or night-clothes, not even a toothbrush ! "

" Never mind," said Martha ; " it's only for a week-end."

The next day they began to prepare for the party. Dr. and Mrs. Brice were coming, and their grown-up daughter Grace, who lived at home. She was a tall girl with prominent teeth, who arranged the flowers in church ; her father said she had housemaid's knee from washing the altar-steps ; and she also scrubbed floors in a military hospital in Adderbury three times a week. Mrs. Brice did a lot of good work in the parish ; and she often used to warn Mrs. Freke against letting Martha work too hard at school. " It will overtax her

Making Conversation

brain," she said. " Now, my brother's child, Cuthbert, was a very clever boy, just like Martha, carrying off all the prizes at school. But they overtaxed his brain, and after he had got a brilliant scholarship to Cambridge, he had a breakdown, and had to take a complete rest. Now he isn't allowed to do anything but make baskets, and they doubt if he'll ever be the same again." Martha was tired of hearing about Cuthbert ; and, anyway, she didn't get any prizes at school, as they were made to give them up because of the war. The children themselves were not consulted, but were given a printed form recording their voluntary sacrifice, and comparing them with the Greeks who were satisfied with crowns of parsley. It ended : " We cultivate beauty without extravagance, in the words of Pericles, Φιλοκαλοῦμεν μετ' εὐτελείας.—Thucydides."

Mr. Lewis, the bank-manager, was coming to the party too, and could be relied on to hand round plates. There was some doubt as to whether the vicar and his

Making Conversation

family should be asked, for the sake of the theologians ; but his family was too large, and he himself was too Low. Audrey and Dorothy Austin were coming, and their brother Bud, who was going to be a solicitor in his father's office. They were a high-spirited and unintelligent family who indulged in every form of sport, and had been given bicycles long before Martha, when they were quite small. Bud was sixteen, Audrey seventeen and a half, and Dorothy fourteen. Audrey was leaving school in the summer, although she had failed in the School Certificate last year, and might again ; she was the girl who was considered too attractive to go for walks with Margaret Hodges. Then there was Alice Lennox, whose grandfather was an old, retired bishop who had been a missionary in South America. He was said to have been the first missionary in the country, and they had a collecting-box at school in the shape of a house, called " Bishop Ingram's House," and one put pennies down the chimney. Long afterwards, Martha discovered

Making Conversation

that there had been Catholic missionaries there before him, and the bishop had spent his time converting papist Indians to protestantism. Alice was strictly brought up by her mother, the bishop's daughter, and never wore whole dresses, but only blouses and skirts, with tight belts around the waist. In the winter she wore yellowing flannel blouses and navy-blue serge skirts; in the summer, cotton blouses and skirts, and in the evening, silk ones; and as she had large hips, it did not suit her. Her hair was in a tight thin plait, tied in a bow at both ends; everything about her seemed to be tight, and her eyes tended to bulge, but she was good-natured. Mr. Lennox had been, or was, " no good," like Major Freke; and that might have drawn Mrs. Lennox and Mrs. Freke together, but did not. The other guests would be Mrs. Drayton's girls, as they were called. Mrs. Drayton was an officer's widow who lived in Adderbury and looked after the children of Anglo-Indians. She had a daughter called Naomi,

Making Conversation

who was so competent that it was impossible to remember she was not grown-up. She had a lovely thick plait tied with satin ribbon, and a velvet band round her head as well ; and her hairdressing was copied by the other girls, Olive Peters and Joyce Dickenson. They wore the same kind of striped ties, too, and red tam o' shanters, and rode about together on bicycles, so that they looked like an institution. Martha always longed to wear a high collar and a tie like a man's, but her mother said it did not suit her because her neck was too short. She could neither plait her hair nor fill it with celluloid combs, but still kept it down with a velvet band. And there was just one good result of the European war, which was that she was allowed to cut off a lot of it.

" You will put on your white to-night, dear, won't you ? " said Mrs. Freke. She meant that Martha ought to put on a white dress for the party.

" Put on my white what ? "

" You know perfectly well what I mean.

Making Conversation

And don't repeat my words; it's a most irritating habit."

" How can I help it, when you're not explicit ? "

" Don't nag. Are you going to wear your white dress to-night ? "

" You know I can't bear my white. It's so terribly *jeune fille*."

" Don't be a little idiot. The time will come when you will want to look younger instead of older than you are."

" Well, it hasn't come yet, and white is very unbecoming when I get hot and shiny, if I'm not allowed to powder my nose."

" You will ruin your skin if you start that at your age, I warn you. And if you put on any more of that disgusting face-cream, it will grow hairs."

CHAPTER VIII

IN the end, Martha put on a summer dress with a pattern of red flowers, which was quite unsuitable to a winter evening, and a red velvet hair-ribbon. Mrs. Freke was in black tulle, and she had provided Madame Michiels with a large embroidered scarf from another Fund. This time it was not a Fund for Serbians or Belgians, but for the Assistance of Reduced Gentlewomen; periodically it sent a parcel of cast-off clothing for her and Martha. Cecil appeared in a dinner-jacket with a deep black stock and white socks. Mrs. Freke wondered if it was good form, when the other poor things hadn't any; but Dragan and Misha had raised some remarkably stiff collars and bow ties, which looked just like evening dress. Monsieur Michiels was as neat as usual.

Rose Amery, a woman from the village, had come in to help with supper and washing-up. The food was mostly sandwiches,

Making Conversation

filled with gritty vegetarian pastes which were very sustaining ; and there was also a *mousse* composed of the meat which had been saved on the family meat-tickets, and of an amount of unregistered entrails. There were chocolate sweets which were really made of cocoa-butter ; and sticks of maple sugar, and fruit-and-nut paste. The drinks were tea and coffee, and lemonade, and cider-cup, made of the local cider and guaranteed harmless.

The family was waiting in the drawing-room for the guests to arrive, when there was a crash in the hall. Martha rushed out and found Brother Velisar slowly descending the stairs, which were badly lighted. Scattered about the floor were broken plates, sandwiches, a tray and the half-swooning form of Rose Amery. She was, in fact, sitting on the floor with her back propped against the wall ; and she was saying, " Oh, Lord ! He've come ! Oh, Lord, have mercy upon me a sinner ! Oh, Lord ! "

Making Conversation

Martha tried to pull her to her feet, and failed; but as Brother Velisar drew nearer, Rose leaped up and ran into the kitchen, where she buried her head in her apron, and was not much use for the rest of the evening.

Mr. Lewis arrived at the front door, and was soon helping to pick up the broken plates. Mrs. Drayton's girls and Alice Lennox came together, and Martha took them all to her bedroom. Alice was wearing a white silk blouse, and an ugly blue skirt in a kind of alpaca; she had shiny white ribbon on her plait. The others wore silk dresses in varying shades of blue, with embroidered white collars and cuffs. Then Audrey and Dorothy came upstairs noisily; Audrey revealed an almost grown-up evening-dress in pale pink satin, and Dorothy was in white. They were both dark and thin and foolish, and made jokes about the foreigners' names.

"They are called Dragoljub and Milenko," said Martha, "but *we* call them Dragan and Misha."

Making Conversation

" Then I shall call them Dragan and Misha, too," said Audrey.

" You can't unless they ask you to," said Martha.

Mrs. Brice and Grace were taking off their things in Mrs. Freke's room. Mrs. Brice was in purple with some trimming called *passementerie* ; she was so small and fat that she seemed unlikely to be the mother of Grace, who was tall and bony, and dressed this evening in yellowish brown. Grace had a bad complexion, and it was not the result of face-cream, which disproved one of Mrs. Freke's theories ; in fact she was a clean, open-air girl and fond of games. Martha thought the spots must be scrum-pox. " Hockey and theophanies," was how the doctor described his daughter's activities, as he was anticlerical and went to church only three times a year. He was a big man with a bald head, who owed a lot of money to the shops, because he did not press his patients to pay their bills. Cecil called Grace ἕρκος ὀδόντων.

Mr. Lewis was playing and singing

Making Conversation

Gilbert and Sullivan downstairs; and as he finished "Take a pair of sparkling eyes," all the refugees applauded enthusiastically. Dragan and Misha and Brother Velisar were sitting together on a sofa. No one knew if they had arranged it beforehand, but suddenly the monk hummed a few notes, and they all burst into song where they sat. It was like nothing anyone had ever heard, except Mrs. Brice, who had been in a Russian church once on the Riviera. "I think it's so wonderful," she said, "how you manage to keep in tune without any organ or harmonium or anything. I used to hear about it from my husband's cousin, too, who was the wife of the vice-consul in Archangel. Do you know Archangel?"

"Oh, no," said Dragan in his deepest and most caressing tones; "I am very sorry." He looked as if he really regretted it.

"What a pity!" said Mrs. Brice. "She was very happy there; of course it was cold, but they had central heating."

Then she jumped slightly, because they

Making Conversation

started again; and this time the song was less religious and more cheerful. After the applause there were sandwiches and coffee. Grace Brice began talking to Misha about Girl Guides, and he was pleased to be noticed. "You can't think," she said, "what a difference it makes to their morale, getting them into uniform." He was telling her about *sokols*, when Dragan went to the piano, and began singing something like "Oom-pa, oom-pa" to a loud, catchy tune. Misha seized Grace's hand and said, "That is *kolo*, Serbian national dance ; we must all dance ! "

Grace blushed scarlet, and tried to copy the complicated things he was doing with his feet.

"It's like an Irish jig," said Mrs. Brice.

"No, it's like a Scotch reel," said Audrey. "We do one like it in dancing-class."

"All dance ! " shouted Misha, and Audrey and Dorothy joined hands with Grace, and did a dancing-class step. Mr. Lewis followed Dorothy, in a step still further removed from Misha's ; and next came

Making Conversation

Mrs. Freke and Martha and Bud. The monk was alone on the sofa, smiling; and the doctor and his wife were talking to the Belgians. The other girls were collected in a corner, talking about school, and Cecil was leaning over the piano. Misha danced up and down the room, with his pupils in a straggling line; whenever he passed the girls who were not dancing, he smiled and shouted at them, but they were terrified and pretended not to notice. He called something to Dragan which must have meant " faster," and they found they were dancing in a circle, with their arms round each other's necks. Martha wondered how Grace felt with Misha's arm round her neck; but Grace was smiling, happy and sweating. When Dragan stopped, they fell panting into chairs, and Cecil, with an ironical smile, gave them lemonade. Mrs. Freke said they must have an English dance, and began to play rag-time.

Misha stayed with Grace, who was very shiny and talking hard. " One, *two*, one, *two*," she said to him, and was delighted

Making Conversation

to get her own back, as he was not good at a fox-trot. Dragan, on the other hand, seemed to have picked up the trick, and was getting on well with Audrey. Mr. Lewis danced with Dorothy and used a pump-handle action for his arm, while allowing his feet to look after themselves. Bud asked Martha to dance, because he had nice manners and thought it was his duty ; but she did not enjoy it, and trod on his feet several times. The four girls in the corner divided into pairs, and began dancing correctly but without animation, as though it were the most natural thing in the world. Alice Lennox and Naomi Drayton " danced man," because they were big and competent. Martha was no good at " dancing man," and indifferent at the usual thing. Dr. and Mrs. Brice danced together, and had evidently been good dancers in the old-fashioned style ; and they left the Michiels and the monk sitting in silence. But not for long.

Before the end of that dance, Brother Velisar rose to his feet, and walked straight

Making Conversation

through the dancers to the door. He looked so pale, severe and ghostlike, that they left a space for him at once. Dragan and Misha dropped their partners and followed him, and there were loud voices in the hall. Grace and Audrey sat down together, betraying traces of that primitive hostility which women feel for each other at dances. When the music stopped, the young men came back, and Dragan explained to Mrs. Freke that the monk did not like English dances, and could not stay in the room while they were going on.

" I'm very sorry," she said, " but I don't see why our dances should be any worse than yours."

" I am so sorry," said Dragan. " It is difficult to explain."

" I quite agree with him," said Cecil. " These dances are American, anyway; and I shall take the responsibility of taking him out myself during the next fox-trot. We shall both be much happier."

" He is Bogumil," said Dragan, and played another *kolo*.

Making Conversation

Mr. Lewis sang again, a comic song called " We've all come up from Zummerzet," which caused Martha acute pain. She was only thankful that she was no longer expected to recite or to play accompaniments. Audrey and Dorothy gave a performance which was almost ballet-dancing, and should have been done in the costumes of a pierrot and pierrette. They learned it in the Close School dancing-class, and it involved a lot of walking about on their toes and kissing hands. It did not outrage the monk's sense of decency, though Cecil was prepared to take him out, and sat at his elbow talking German. Martha thought the dance stupid and pointless, but everyone clapped hard. After it they all went into the dining-room for the *mousse* and more sandwiches and sweets and the cider-cup ; and Cecil stayed there with the monk and the Michiels, while Mrs. Freke risked some more fox-trots.

During an interval, she sent Martha to look for another jug of cider-cup, which

Making Conversation

might be on the table in the smoking-room. This was the small room under the bathroom, which contained only a sofa, a writing-table and one chair, and a bookcase. It had not even a fireplace, as it was warmed by the hot-water pipes. The door was shut, but Martha opened it and saw that two people were sitting on the sofa which was against the wall to the left. They were Audrey and Dragan, and they were kissing each other. Martha shut the door again quickly, and went back to tell her mother there was no more cider-cup. She had a dentist-feeling in her stomach from shock and jealousy; and she was at the same time wildly excited and full of theories. In the first place, it was contemptible of Dragan to be taken in by such an inferior creature as Audrey; but in the second place, this was Life, seen at first hand and not in novels; and all her principles as an enlightened and freethinking woman prevented her from saying anything about it. What was hardest to believe was that they found any pleasure

Making Conversation

in it; there was nothing more boring than being kissed by aunts, uncles and demonstrative women; but Dragan and Audrey evidently enjoyed it, and were inflamed by a genuine passion. This was an object lesson, on the danger of being cut out by stupid, pretty girls. It must be the question of conversation again, and Martha always found herself fluctuating between talking too little and too much. She began to wonder if they were really in love, and if Audrey would marry him and go and live in Beograd; but she decided to shield them, whatever happened. They might not have noticed her opening the door, and she would wait until one of them said something about it.

She had not even looked for the jug of cup; but it was quite true that it was not there, and in fact, there was no more cider either. Mrs. Freke began to have her suspicions when Monsieur Michiels held Mrs. Brice's hand for a long time saying good night. He seemed to cling to it as if it gave him support, which was surprising,

Making Conversation

as it was a small podgy hand, and she was a small woman. When all the guests had gone, Madame Michiels crossed the room diagonally from her corner, and she was not quite steady either. She put her face close to Mrs. Freke's (" And I could smell her distinctly," said Mrs. Freke later), and said with a smile, " My husband, madame, he is a little drunk."

" Yes, madame," said Monsieur, " I am a little drunk." He took his wife's arm, and they seemed positively proud of it.

" Yes," said Misha coldly, " they are drunk."

Martha noticed that Dragan was still outside saying good-bye to someone ; and she was seething with emotions.

" Nonsense ! " said Mrs. Freke. " He is only a little excited, and you are both tired. You must go to bed."

" I tell you, madame," said Monsieur assertively, " I am *drunk* ! "

There is always a panic among sober people when drunks show signs of being even a little quarrelsome. " Very well,

Making Conversation

monsieur," said Mrs. Freke, in a soothing tone; " all the more reason for going to bed."

" I don't go to bed, madame, until you say good night to me ! "

" Gustave ! " said his wife sharply.

He repeated over Mrs. Freke's hand the ceremony he had performed over Mrs. Brice's, but at even greater length. Then he swayed in the direction of Brother Velisar, and before he could be stopped, pulled the monk's beard. Then he slapped him on the back and said, " *Bon soir, Raspoutine !* " As he ascended the stairs with his wife, he told her some obscene stories about the habits of monks.

That night in bed, Martha felt that she had come to the end of a period in her life. She was thinking of Dragan and Audrey. It was more staggering than when she had heard what Harry thought of her ; for that was a purely intellectual affair, and there was something to be said on his side. She had recognised that he was right, and that her intellectual interests had not gone so

Making Conversation

deep as her desire to please; and she had been unhappy at being found out. But this time she was more furiously angry than she was unhappy; and she found a certain satisfaction in martyrdom. After all she had done for Dragan! She had maintained her spiritual integrity, and insisted on the importance of literary criticism, when she easily might have given in. And after all those walks on the New Road, he had kissed one of her friends without a word of warning. He might at least have told her that he liked Audrey, and she would have been sympathetic. She could imagine herself carrying notes for the clandestine lovers, providing disguises to assist an elopement, and making any sacrifice, like the girl-friend in the story of Tristan and Yseult. But they hadn't let her into their confidence.

It was true that Dragan had applauded Audrey's pierrot dance, but Martha couldn't believe he really admired it. It was a mistake to underrate the forces of passion, and one must keep one's eyes open.

Making Conversation

It made her feel more Bogumil than ever: Audrey and Dragan on the sofa, and Monsieur and Madame staggering with cider-cup were deplorably carnal. She would renounce all the lusts of the flesh. It would save a lot of trouble, and as she wasn't a success on the carnal side, she might as well give it up. In that case, there would be no need to marry and have a family; and she could become famous as a Homeric scholar. Just as she turned over to go to sleep, she remembered a rather good essay she had written about the Renaissance, about living a life that was complete physically and mentally, and how Ronsard grew his own vegetables. The love-poems of Ronsard were divine. There was the one in the *Hundred Best Poems* and all the other anthologies, beginning " *Mignonne, allons voir si la rose.*" If one gave up the lusts of the flesh, one would have to give up that too. Never mind, it couldn't be helped. And Brother Velisar was right about dancing.

CHAPTER IX

IT was taken for granted that Martha would go to Oxford. In the days of Mr. Pyggott's pupils, the whole of life had seemed to her to be preparation for a university. To " get in " was like getting into heaven. But whereas for the Chileans and Mauritians it was a place where one hoped to lead the life of a gentleman, for Martha it was a place where one finally proved how clever one was. Nothing could be more delightful. It would be a nursery of independent thought and intellectual aristocracy, of brilliant young men of every race, and advanced young women who asserted their equality with them. At school, too, the tone of the Upper Sixth was set by the entrance examinations to the women's colleges. Girls who were as stupid as Audrey Austin never got beyond the Lower Sixth ; they just left school and went home. But girls in the Upper Sixth were

Making Conversation

set apart and distinguished by their future purpose, like candidates for ordination.

" That's Martha Freke ; she's doing classics. She's going to Oxford."

" That's Mary Entwhistle ; she's going to Girton."

" What's she doing ? "

" History."

" Is she good ? "

" Rather ! Her sister got a schol last year."

So in the spring of 1918, Martha went to Oxford for the scholarship examination at Springfield College. She wore a new navy-blue coat-and-skirt and a blue straw hat ; and she took a new mackintosh, and some clean shirt-blouses, and a navy-blue " coat-frock," which was a fashion of that year, and a mauve shantung dress for the evenings. She changed trains at Bristol with complete sang-froid, as she knew the station, which smelt of fish. She had been to Christmas pantomimes and Benson's Shakespeare in the Prince's Theatre.

As the train came into Oxford, she looked

Making Conversation

out for dreaming spires in the twilight, and was not disappointed. Hansom-cabs intensified the atmosphere, and to ride in one was a new and invigorating sensation. The streets near the station were depressing, of course ; then there were some shops ; and then, as she was expecting to be set down in the shadow of a dreaming spire, there were suburbs. Just as she was succumbing to a reaction of disappointment, the cab stopped at a big door, which had a little door inside it, like Adderbury Prison. She paid the driver several shillings and a tip, and stood on the pavement with her suitcase, umbrella and mackintosh, and with the feeling in the pit of her stomach which she usually had outside doors, since the High School.

A friendly man appeared in shirt-sleeves and an apron, and said, " This all you got, miss ? " and " What name, miss ? " She said, " Freke, F-R-E-K-E," and he wrote it in a book, and took her up a long path to a building which was quite lacking in spires. Inside the front door was a hall

Making Conversation

where a lot of girls were standing and talking, or reading notices on the walls. They all seemed very mature, with their hair up and long skirts, and they wore the kind of afternoon dresses which one wears in the evening. A small girl with rimless eyeglasses, who seemed no older than the rest, darted at Martha, and said she had better go to her room, and needn't change for dinner as it was too late, and she could see Miss Gregory after dinner. Miss Gregory was the principal.

A fat woman in black velvet, who looked about forty, said, " That's Freke, isn't it ? Come along, I'll show you your room." She took Martha's arm, a gesture which always made her feel awkward, as did all demonstrations of affection. In the first place, it was hard to keep in step, and the other woman's hips rubbed against one uncomfortably. Also, the person whose arm is taken is in a definitely inferior position to the person who takes it, and looks silly. It is difficult to find any way of expressing one's gratitude, except by feverish

Making Conversation

conversation. The woman in black smelled of sweat, which reminded Martha of life in institutions, of the cloak-room at the High School, and games and drill. She disliked contact with a herd ; and since Cecil had given her a translation of *The Dawn of Day*, she had become a Nietzschean aristocrat. It was inscribed, " To Martha Freke. March on in the light of the Great Dawn. *Verum impendere vitæ*. With this book I open my campaign against morality."

The woman in black said, " I'm Tinker. I was up for a schol last year, so I know what it feels like."

Martha could think of nothing but " Oh, were you really ? "

" Yes, I'm only a fresher. We stayed up after term to work ; a little nest of us."

What a horrid metaphor ; but Miss Tinker was very kind. Poor Miss Tinker ; with such a name, no wonder she dropped the " Miss." Perhaps she wasn't so old after all. They had walked along a gravel path to another building, and a swing door let them into a corridor.

Making Conversation

"You're in Thompson's room," said Tinker. "I don't expect she left anything in the chest-of-drawers. She only has one blouse, which she washes herself, and when she wants a change, she Twinks it." This was followed by a hearty laugh, and must be a joke.

The room was small and cold. It contained an iron bed with an Indian printed bed-spread; a chest-of-drawers with a small mirror hanging on a nail above it; a table and a small chair; a big basket-chair by the fireplace; a wardrobe of stained oak, and a washstand behind a Japanese paper screen. The floor was stained, with a rug in the middle. The walls were distempered cream; over the mantelpiece was a Medici print of Botticelli's "Spring"; and there was a rhyme-sheet pinned to the door with drawing-pins.

"There's a coal shortage," said Tinker, "so we club together and save it as much as we can. Some of us are having a little binge to-night, so come along after seeing the Greg." She bundled Martha back to

Making Conversation

the front hall, and from there to the dining-hall. They sat next to a woman called Porter, with a black ribbon round her head and a large bun of hair, who looked like Grace Brice. But it made a difference that Miss Porter must have a brain, and Grace hadn't ; the time that Miss Porter saved on beauty-culture, she must devote to scholarship, and one could respect her for that. There were, after all, some younger girls with pigtails. There was an Indian woman with a silk thing over her head, and some obvious Jewesses and noisy Americans. The women at the High Table were dons, and Tinker and Porter referred to them by nicknames. The Greg was a tall, imposing woman in grey silk, with hair arranged in a solid halo in the manner of Miss Pilkington, the Frekes' late paying-guest. Sitting next her was Miss Monkhouse.

" That's the Monk. She's like a pug dog, isn't she ? " said Porter. " The one on the other side is Smack. Miss Macdonald. She's the one who'll deal with you. She's very Scotch."

Making Conversation

That one was certainly bony, with high cheek-bones and a vivid complexion; she wore a large Cairngorm brooch on a pre-Raphaelitish dress of a mulberry shade. More definitely arty was a dark young woman in green velvet with a high waist, called the Taylor. The small person with eyeglasses who had greeted Martha was the Greg's secretary; and a normal-looking woman was the bursar, the Cart, or Miss Cartwright.

" She's a good sort," said Tinker, " and does the best she can with our food-tickets. The food might be a lot worse."

" I never mind what food is like," said Porter, " as long as there's plenty of it."

Dinner started with clear soup, which was clear enough, but hardly soup; next came minced mutton, boiled potatoes which had been put through a mincing machine and had come out in flakes like rice, but black in places (which showed they were potatoes still); and mashed yellow turnips; and a hot chocolate sweet, which could not

Making Conversation

be expected to be very sweet, and revealed the familiar taste of cocoa-butter.

" A good lot of people up for schols," said Porter.

" And there are a lot of Scotch ones doing it at home," said Tinker. " There are some very good people at St. Mungo's this year." That meant that even if Martha was better than all the people here, she had unseen enemies. It was an unpleasant thought that in this conglomeration of young women (apart from Tinker and Porter and the nest of students), everyone's hand was against everyone. The more people were " good," the less chance one had. They were like animals in the jungle, as they sat gobbling their chocolate-pudding.

" Have you got the wind up about to-morrow ? " asked Porter kindly.

" Oh, not at all," said Martha, meaning to be polite, and then realised that it sounded conceited. " Yes, of course I have rather." There was an awkward pause, as the two first-year students looked at each

Making Conversation

other significantly. Martha made it worse by beginning to talk.

" Those dons look like the gods of the Epicureans, don't they ? " She didn't wait for an answer, but went on rapidly, " Nietzsche said that if one was a god, one would find a lot of human activities very irritating, and especially human marriage. But at least there isn't any fear of that in a community like this." Still no answer, and she went on, " I think the Epicurean theory of God is quite the most attractive, and gives one least trouble in ordinary life." But just then dinner came to an end ; and after a small cup of coffee, which tasted as it does in institutions, she found herself outside the principal's door, with the usual feeling.

" Come in," said a bright voice, and she walked into a large room, which was in some ways like Thompson's bed-sitting-room, though more imposing. There was the same lack of unnecessary furniture ; the same polished floor, only it was parquet instead of boards, and the rugs were better.

Making Conversation

There were some coldish engravings on the walls, which were distempered light grey.

"Now, Miss Freke, you are up for a scholarship, I think."

"Yes, Miss Gregory." It was funny to be called Miss, after being called by one's Christian name at school; there were so many Misses in this place, it was no wonder they tended to use surnames only.

Now, some of the scholarships were reserved for candidates who needed financial help and were going to take up teaching; and Martha had a conscience about it, as she had no leanings to that profession. But Miss Gregory made it easy for her by saying, "And are you going to earn your living?"—in a firm voice—" And teach?"—in a less determined tone. It suggested that the two courses were identical, so she said, "Yes," with a mental reservation.

"And you are at the Close School, Adderbury." Miss Gregory remembered the name of this not very famous school with a bright smile, as the Royal Family might remember an engine-driver.

Making Conversation

" And what are your main interests in the classics ? "

" Mainly literary," said Martha.

Miss Gregory smiled brilliantly and waited.

" I am very fond of lyric poetry," said Martha, and blushed because it sounded idiotic. " Catullus," she went on, attempting to explain, and stopped.

" I see. And are you interested in ancient history ? "

" Oh, yes ! " (She knew that she had a bad habit of saying, " *Oh*, yes " and " *Oh*, no," which would probably tell against her.) " Especially the later period of Roman history," she went on quickly. " Tacitus, for instance. I prefer history when it comes through the medium of a great literary artist."

" I see. And Greek history, Miss Freke ? "

" Oh, I like Herodotos very much, there is so much more colour in him than in Thucydides."

" I see. And are you interested in archæology ? "

Making Conversation

"Oh, yes!" Then a silence, while she felt like a fool.

"Are you at all interested in the problems of modern warfare on ancient sites?"

"Oh, yes!" But it must be evident from her face that she was telling a lie, and she took it back. "Well, as a matter of fact——" (Miss Spencer at the High School had always scolded her for saying "well," and used to ask, "Where's the bucket?") "As a matter of fact, I am not interested in modern warfare."

"I see. Now, Miss Freke, what are your other interests, beyond literature?"

"Well, I really don't know!"

"Are you interested in music?"

"Oh, yes, but not to do anything myself."

"Dancing?"

"Oh, no!" Memories of that awful party rushed into her mind. "Well, at least, as an art possibly, but I'm afraid I've never seen the Russian Ballet," she said apologetically. She had only heard about it from Cecil.

Making Conversation

" The theatre ? " with a smile.

" Oh, yes," vaguely.

" The graphic arts ? "

Martha was uneasy, as she wasn't sure how many these included.

" Oh, yes," she said, " I am interested in modern art, and in the general principles of æsthetics." Then she blushed violently again, as the last phrase came out of the *Times Literary Supplement*.

" Games ? " asked Miss Gregory, who had become a Cheshire cat.

" Oh, no ! " said Martha firmly.

Miss Gregory rose to her feet and said good night and that she hoped Martha would like her papers. How could one possibly like examination-papers ? At the end of miles of corridor she found Tinker's room ; and Tinker was in a pantry outside, boiling a kettle on a gas-ring. Inside, a lot of women were talking and laughing, including Porter and one of the Indians. Someone threw a cushion on the floor and said, " Will you squat ? "

" How did you get on with the Greg ? "

Making Conversation

asked Porter, and Martha said she didn't know.

" Smack is a lot worse," said a girl who was sitting on the bed. " She'll ask if you're fond of bike-rides, and if you are, she'll take you out on Ark."

" What's Ark ? "

" The Springfield College Archæological Society."

Martha thought of archæology in terms of Homeric scholarship rather than of bicycles.

" But she may be away still when you come up, or *if* you come up " (how tactless). " She's doing warr-worrk " (this in a Scotch accent) " at the Foreign Office. She's democratising diplomacy, or diplomatising democracy, or something." Loud laughter.

" Do you know the story about her and Dr. Blumenfeld ? " asked Porter.

The nest of first-years evidently did, but she told it for the sake of the scholarship candidates. " Well, old Blumenfeld—I'm sorry, I mean Bloomfield, but that was his

Making Conversation

name before the war, when my brother was up." Loud laughter again. Martha wondered if it was due to " Comb out the Huns " sentiment, or a proper contempt for a German who denied his name. " Well, old Blumenfeld came up one morning in the Summer Term for an early tutorial, and Smack had been sleeping out and had overslept." Shouts of laughter. " History does not relate," said Porter, " whether she was snoring or not, but from personal experience of sleeping near her, I should say she was." More laughter. " He was on his famous bicycle, of course, and as he was thinking about the Absolute or something, and she was on the path, he rode right over her." Everyone screamed and shouted, and there was one girl who even wheezed. The scholarship candidates thought this was the end of the story, but Tinker and some others knew better, and saved their loudest screams for the climax. " Well, Smack picked herself up spluttering, and dragged her bed on to the grass, and old Bloomers went to give his tutorial.

Making Conversation

And on the way back he remembered what had happened before, so he rode across the grass, and rode over her again."

The cocoa-party rocked and swayed with laughter; then there was an awkward silence, before anyone could think of another story. Martha knew she must not open her mouth. There was a girl sitting on one of the things called "poufs" or "humpties," in a black taffeta dress with a wide skirt which spread over the floor. She had dark hair in heavy flaps on her ears and forehead, and a face like a small monkey's, which would always be sensuously attractive, even when her nose was shiny, as it was at the moment. She was blowing rings of cigarette-smoke with an air of intensity, and began to talk. "He couldn't have been thinking about the Absolute, because he's its most deadly enemy."

"Well, you ought to know," said Tinker. "Miss Stubbs is a third-year doing Greats," she explained to the scholarship candidates. "She is a superior being to us,

Making Conversation

and it is very kind of her to grace this party with her presence."

They were not quite sure whether this was a joke, but when Tinker herself laughed heartily, they joined.

"I wonder why most Greats women look so awful," said Miss Stubbs. "I don't know if it is cause or effect." This was so brilliant that no one could keep pace with it. "But at least," she went on, "ours aren't so bad as the ones at St. Tubno's."

"Do you know what they say about women-students' clothes?" asked Porter, who evidently had another story. "They say that S.D.H. are tailor-made" (laughter), "we are ready-made" (more laughter), "and St. Tubno's are *home-made*!" Shouts of laughter.

"What are S.D.H.?" asked the Indian woman.

"St. Dymphna's Hall," said Tinker. "They think they're very swish."

"Quite an unfounded assumption," said Miss Stubbs. "It doesn't work. Unlike Bloomers' bicycle. By the way, did you see

Making Conversation

that perfectly screaming thing in the *Cher* last week?"

They hadn't, so she went on, "It was illustrating Bloomers' Theory of Knowledge. Bloomers pedalling along on his old bike, saying, ' It's true, because it works'!"

There was an awkward silence, then some uneasy laughter.

"That's pragmatism, you know," explained Miss Stubbs kindly, "or a jolly good rag of it."

"Now," said Tinker, "if you could get him and Smack on their bikes together, you could make a record score in ' Beaver.' One black beaver on bicycle, with one red female beaver on bicycle. Oh, Lord!" Everyone laughed again.

"You could easily get her with Dr. Peshitch," said Porter. "They say she's teaching him to ride one. She puts him on top of a hill in the Chilterns and just sends him off. Oh, my hat!"

"He's one of ' My Montenegrins,' as she calls them," said Miss Stubbs, "and she adores him. Annie in the lodge says

Making Conversation

he's a dream." Martha recognised a note of contempt for small nations.

" Oh, but did you hear the latest ? " asked Porter.

" No, my dear. *What?* "

" About Smack's G.P. for the Taylor ? "

" Shut up ! " said Tinker, and asked Martha if she was keen on hockey.

" I'm afraid I'm no good at it," said Martha, as politely as possible.

" It doesn't matter so much about being good," said Tinker. " I don't know about present company. We're not *good*, but we're *keen*."

" There ought to be some players coming on at St. Mungo's," said Porter, " and what about Holmlea ? "

Martha and the Indian woman were the only people in the room who had not heard about Holmlea. Heads began to turn towards a big girl in navy blue, who was sitting on the floor. She had a red, spotty face and straight dark hair, which was supposed to be done up in a bun, but was coming down.

Making Conversation

" I don't know," she said, in a deep voice. " Hogg and Heard are going to Cambridge, and Witherstone-Bulley had 'flu and scratched the entrance. But there's always a Titmuss or two coming on."

" Good," said Tinker, in a voice which had sunk to the same pitch. " I don't know what college would do without the Titmusses."

" Titmice," suggested Miss Stubbs, and several people threw cushions at her. The fire was burning low, and the party broke up. Thompson's room was cold and smelt odd, and Martha did not wash much, for fear of splashing the screen.

Next morning she woke early, but lay stiff with terror until quite late. There was someone in the bathroom, so she tried to wash in and from the basin. At eight o'clock she began to hurry down the corridor, and found a misty morning at the end of it; but once in the open air, she was lost again. The hall must be in a large building with uniform windows some distance off, and she ran towards it self-consciously and ungracefully, as girls of seventeen run if they are not lacrosse players, and sometimes even if they are. But no, this staircase was spiral, and it had not been last night. Perhaps her head was going round, or perhaps this was a nightmare and she was still asleep. It needed less courage to go on than back, and at the top she found a dim passage lined with books, and a house-maid on her knees.

" Please could you tell me the way to the hall ? "

" Back down the stairs, miss, and over there," said the maid, pointing in the direction from which Martha had come. She ran back, hitching up her navy-blue skirt and pushing down her white shirt-blouse, with spiral stairs of fright twisting in her brain. Then she saw a little door which led to another staircase, with a swing door at the top. It did not swing very well and had to be pushed hard ; but just as she was in despair, she found herself in the passage outside the hall. Through a sheet of glass she saw dishes on a metal counter,

Making Conversation

and beyond that the backs of women kneeling. They were praying. As they floundered to their feet, she dared to push another swing door, and inserted herself into a queue for breakfast. She was making for a plate of scrambled eggs, when a hand was pressed on her shoulder. It was Miss Stubbs, who said, " Don't! They are not what they seem! "

" Oh, really ? "

" No, they are Farm Eggs, which means Egg Powder, which means Custard Powder, which means *Custard Pudding*."

The thought of custard pudding can curdle one's blood at ten minutes past eight in the morning; and Martha had little appetite for the kipper which she found instead, for which no fish-knives were provided. She ate a little bread and margarine and swede jam, and drank some institutional coffee. She had not noticed a toast-rack in front of her when she heard Porter's voice, " Is that your little nest of toast, Miss Freke ? " How that girl loved the word " nest "; and she was going on,

Making Conversation

" You are looking so cosy there, it seems a shame to bag it."

Martha staggered out to have an interview with the classical tutor, Miss Macdonald. She was certainly a red beaver. Her room had the usual plain walls, stained floor, and rugs ; but the pictures were photographs of ancient monuments, and on the mantelpiece were some reproductions of Minoan treasures. There was something Minoan about her waist, which was unnaturally small, and in her colouring there was a crude, archaic beauty. Her voice was inhuman as she enquired name, school, and books read in Latin and Greek. It was soon over, and Martha found her way back to the hall, which still smelt of breakfast, for a General Paper. She wrote an emotional answer on Latin literature of the Silver Age, bringing in the phrase " a subtle odour of decay."

Lunch brought with it a new smell. It was a choice between cold mutton and two kinds of rice, of which one was coloured pink and might contain tomatoes, while

Making Conversation

the other was yellow and might be connected with custard pudding. There were potatoes baked in their skins, and boiled greens ; and afterwards, suet puddings or milk puddings mixed with watery jam. The scholarship candidates discussed their papers. " I think the General's easiest." " I'd always rather have an Unseen." " An Unseen's all right unless you get stuck."

After lunch they had an English essay, and Martha wrote four and a half foolscap pages on " Art and Life," bringing in the quotation :

> *Oui, l'œuvre sort plus belle*
> *D'une forme au travail*
>   *Rebelle,*
> *Vers, marbre, onyx, émail.*

The next day came a Latin prose and a Greek Unseen, and the day after, a Latin Unseen and a Greek prose, and then they went home.

CHAPTER X

MARTHA was not surprised to hear that she had been given a scholarship. It was announced in school, and everyone clapped. That summer she lived in the future. Dragan and Misha were boarded out at Bexhill by the Fund. Cecil wrote her a letter of congratulation from Rome. Goodness knows how he had managed to get his passport visa'd, it must have been the influence of his illegitimate family.

" My dear Child "—he said—" Permit me to offer you my best wishes on your precocious attainment. I hope it will not lead you on to a stagnant life in the quiet of some Springfield cell, but will rather broaden your efforts, and that you will remember ' Shakespeare was of us, Byron was for us, Shelley was with us,' and so on. *Don't* have any pictures in your room, or if you must, a

Making Conversation

few in the bedroom. Or don't you have two rooms ? And *don't* have any patterns on your cushions. One of the easiest ways to give ' style ' to a room, in these days of stylelessness, is, I find, to eliminate all patterns. Rome is too grand for one to do anything. What can one do, one says, that will equal this or that ? If Queen Elizabeth had paid Shakespeare's passage to Rome, he would never have written *Julius Cæsar*. *Julius Cæsar* is more like Rome, *the* Rome, than Rome is. At night, one can sometimes get that Rome ; but in the daytime it is all Piranesi and Goethe. Do you know Piranesi ? Love from

" CECIL."

Uncle Randolph saw Martha's scholarship announced in *The Times*, and so did a lot of other relations and friends who were in the habit of reading *The Times* all through, and of never bothering about the Frekes. Mrs. Freke bought Martha some new clothes, including a blue and a pink

Making Conversation

afternoon-dress to wear at dinner, and a real evening-dress as well, with a low neck back and front, and short, transparent sleeves. The low neck was an agony to Martha, but her mother and the dressmaker said it was quite all right.

So in October she went to Oxford, where her first impressions were of autumn leaves, and of mist at the end of every street. She brought with her a black rug for her bed, and black curtains to conceal her wash-stand; some lengths of orange sateen for the mantelpiece and chest-of-drawers, and a Liberty silk handkerchief for the table; cushions in plain sateen covers of red, yellow and orange; some German reproductions of Cézanne; and a plaster cast of a head of Alexander the Great, for which there was no place except on the wardrobe. Her room was a small one on the ground floor.

Miss Gregory was very kind when she went for an interview, and asked how she was settling in. " Did you bring much with you, Miss Freke ? "

Making Conversation

"No, Miss Gregory. The biggest thing I brought was a head of Alexander the Great."

"Really? How interesting. And *why* Alexander the Great?"

This was where Martha's powers of conversation gave way. She might have said, "Why not?" or explained that he was a superman, and the most attractive character in ancient history; that he had an unparalleled influence on the art of his time; and that she wouldn't have had Julius Cæsar for anything, as he was too obvious, and, anyway, the usual portrait of him wasn't authentic. But instead she said, "I don't know; I happened to have him by me"; though she had written to the British Museum specially, and paid two guineas for the cast out of her own money.

Miss Macdonald was interviewing all the first-year classical students together. One was a cow-like girl with spectacles and a fine complexion, wearing a white shirt-blouse and a tie with club colours; the two others were nondescript and dressed in tweeds, with felt hats pulled firmly over their faces.

"I must explain," said Miss Macdonald, "that I am returning to London immediately, and leaving you in charge of Mr. Barrington-Ramsbotham of St. Jude's College, whose services we have been fortunate enough to procure. But I should like to settle your Prepared Books. Have you any preferences as regards a Greek book, Miss Freke?"

"Pindar," said Martha.

"Pindar," said Miss Macdonald, "is not educational. Considering the disabilities under which women students always labour, I should recommend you to choose a prose book."

The next interview was with Mr. Barrington-Ramsbotham, whose name made them giggle; and the fact that he was quite a young man made them giggle still more. He was a war-hero, and his appointment had been made, not only on grounds of scholarship, but also because he had "seen life." He was small and blond, with a

Making Conversation

tooth brush moustache and a rich voice. It seemed that the cow-like girl was called Parker, and the others were Spragge and Dobbie.

"I'm sure a prose book is *safer*," said Parker, as they came away.

"Can't we do as we like, now we've left school?" asked Spragge with passion. "Even if Pindar did write in vain for Miss Macdonald."

"Oh, she isn't so bad," said the cow. "She's only Scotch."

"So am I," exploded Dobbie.

"Perhaps Mr. Ramsbotham will be nicer," said Spragge.

"He looks like a sumpf," said Dobbie.

"I think he's rather sweet," said Spragge.

That night the College assembled in the Junior Common Room, and the students huddled behind each other, to avoid the dons as they picked their partners for dinner at the High Table. Then they filed upstairs to the Hall, two by two and some arm-in-arm. The first-years sat together, and the second-years together, and the

Making Conversation

third- and fourth-years together. The new students looked crude and agitated, the second-years were most talkative, and the third-years mature and disillusioned. As the clear soup was being handed around, two girls walked in self-consciously and stood for some time in front of the High Table until they caught Miss Gregory's eye. She bowed slightly, and they went to their places. It was the penalty of being late.

After dinner, Martha and Spragge and Dobbie all went to cocoa with Miss Bateman and Miss Robinson, who were second-years. They both had black velvet ribbons round their heads, and one was rather pretty but spotty-faced. " You're from St. Mungo's, aren't you ? " she said to Spragge. " I've heard about you from Tinker."

" Tinker's a marvel," said the other. " She's good at everything. She'll be taking you out in *Rowena*."

" What's Rowena ? " asked another fresher.

" She's the boat you have to go out in to pass the sculling-test."

Making Conversation

"Does anyone ever not pass the sculling-test?"

"Oh, no one who is keen. After all, it's one of the best things about this place, that you learn how to manage a boat. Do you want any more sugar? Because if you do, there isn't any. It was in the Ideal Milk." There were shouts of laughter.

"And it's Rowntree's Breakfast Chocolate," said a fat girl in a high-waisted dress of juvenile cut. "Do you remember when we had Cadbury to cocoa? I said, 'I'm sorry, Miss Cadbury, it's only Rowntree's!'" Loud laughter.

"Do you know," said the second-year who was probably Bateman, "that Hodgkinson has a passion for Ideal Milk? She may be discovered eating it from a spoon at dead of night." Laughter again. "And Smack has a passion for digestive biscuits. Do you know the story about her and old Bloomfield?"

After that came the story of an American student and some fudge; and next, the story of the Jewess and the cinnamon

Making Conversation

lozenges; and then the story of the æsthete and the lemons. "When they asked him what the lemons were for, he said, 'Just to look at; they are so beautiful.' And another one said, when he had some people to tea, 'I can never hope to live up to my blue china.' And there was another who said the only thing worth producing in life was a purple mist."

"Surely all those stories were told about Oscar Wilde," said Martha.

"They were told when daddy was up," said Dobbie in a high-pitched Scotch voice, "and they're told at Cambridge and Edinburgh and Glasgow and Trinity College, Dublin."

There was an awkward silence. "I think we've been talking too much," said Martha, as they came away at 10 o'clock. They went to her room, where they found a woman in navy-blue silk with hair in plaits round her head and rimless eyeglasses.

"I'm Legge," she said; "I've come about the S.C.C.F."

Making Conversation

"Thank you very much," said Martha. "How kind of you."

"You will all join, won't you?" said Legge.

"Join what?"

"The S.C.C.F. The Springfield College Christian Fellowship."

"Oh, thank you very much. But I'm not sure of my position with regard to the Christian religion. In fact, I'm not sure I'm a Christian." Martha realised this was a crisis; hard though it was to disagree with people, it had to be done.

"That doesn't matter," said Legge brightly. "We're on a very broad basis. We have quite a little corner in agnostics. We don't believe in dogma."

"Surely," said Miss Dobbie, "dogma is quite essential to religion. A religion without dogma is like a parcel tied up without any string."

"I think," said Miss Spragge, "that religion is a matter of revelation. Either you have a revelation or you haven't. It must be wonderful. I haven't had one, but

Making Conversation

I'm prepared to recognise it when it comes. How fortunate you are."

Miss Legge was embarrassed.

"Yes," said Martha, "religion is a matter of mysticism and not logic. I think religions ought to be as mystical and obscurantist as possible. But in that case, mystics are the last people who ought to enjoy each other's society. It's so—subjective. They ought to walk alone, like the rhinoceros."

The others tittered, except Miss Legge, who changed her ground. "On the contrary," she said, " it's the social side which we enjoy. It's very well developed. We have study circles and discussion groups. And we have an annual conference in the summer in the Lake District, where people who *think* can really get together. Tennis and tramping in the daytime, and discussion in the evening. It's the atmosphere that counts. Why, you can see a bishop playing tennis in shorts, just like one of ourselves."

"How jolly," said someone.

Making Conversation

" We have discussions with Jews and Mahommedans, who are associate members. Some people even want to bring in Buddhists."

" Oh, why not ? " asked Miss Spragge.

" I'm against Buddhists myself," said Miss Legge. " One has to draw the line somewhere."

Miss Dobbie lighted a cigarette.

" What a pity," said Miss Spragge suddenly, " that no one can discover a really new drug ! "

Miss Legge jumped, said she would send them some literature, and went out.

" Darling," said Spragge to Dobbie, " will you teach me how to smoke ? And may I call you by your Christian name ? Mine's Elizabeth."

" Mine's Helen."

" This is called ' propping,' " continued Elizabeth, " Evelyn Tinker told me. It's derived either from ' proposing ' or from ' proper ' names. We must never do it to second-years, but in our second term they may do it to us." She put a cigarette in her

Making Conversation

mouth, puffed, panted and blew out the light Helen held for her. There was another knock at the door, and another girl with rimless eyeglasses came in. " Hullo ! " she said. " Would you like to join the New Conservatives ? "

" I don't know," said Martha ; " I don't think I'm a Conservative."

" Is it the same as the Primrose League ? " asked Elizabeth.

" Oh, no, it's on a very broad basis. You can belong to any school of thought and subscribe to it at the same time. It's mainly for purposes of discussion, and we have discussion groups and study circles. Tinker is a very active member. We have quite a corner in Tory democrats."

" Thank you very much," said Martha ; " but I think I'm a revolutionary and not a democrat."

" I'm a Scottish Separatist," said Helen.

" So'm I," said Elizabeth.

" Really ? " said the Conservative woman. " I didn't know you were Scotch too."

Making Conversation

"No, but I was at school at St. Mungo's."

The woman went out, and another came in who wore a navy-blue flannel blazer over a black silk dress. She had a large nose and hardly any chin. "I came to ask you," she said, "to join the S.W.F."

"No, thank you," said Elizabeth quickly, but Martha asked what it stood for.

"The Society for Women's Freedom. You know it used to be the Society for Women's Suffrage, then they gave women the vote, and we changed the name."

"So why does it still go on?" asked Helen.

"Oh, the object of it is mainly social. It runs study circles and discussion groups, and it educates women in politics."

"I think," said Helen, "that if there is one thing the English should wish to keep dark, it's their politics."

There was a silence, which Martha broke. "Thank you very much," she said, and giggled; "but I'm afraid I'm a reactionary. I agree with Nietzsche that

Making Conversation

man was made for war and woman for the enjoyment of the warrior."

Elizabeth laughed, swallowed some cigarette smoke and choked, and the woman went.

CHAPTER XI

NEXT morning there were kippers for breakfast. " If you went up to the High," said a woman in a blazer, " you would get two forks to eat them with, and you might get real butter."

" But we're not supposed to go up there, are we ? " asked a fresher who was on her guard against practical jokes.

" Yes, we're supposed to go up periodically and give the S.C.R. its breakfast. They hate it as much as we do. Good college women go up about once a week."

"I never speak to anyone at breakfast,"said Helen, who had a lot of powder on her face.

After breakfast they went shopping, and bought Elizabeth some powder and face-cream, as she hadn't any. " We must give you some ear-flaps too, dear," said Helen. " It's indecent to show your ears like that."

" We weren't allowed to cover them at St. Mungo's," said Elizabeth.

In Cornmarket Street they saw Bateman

Making Conversation

and Robinson, who made no sign of recognition, and at Carfax they saw the Christian Miss Legge, who cut them, too. In a china-shop, however, they were recognised by Parker, who was rejecting a tea-service she didn't like. " I don't think," she was saying, " that those are the kind of cups one would like to live with. I like something a bit subdued."

" Tea-cups," said Helen, " are not to be lived with, but to be lived up to. Surely you know that, Miss Parker."

Tinker and Porter came out of the hardware department.

" Evelyn," said Elizabeth, " I do believe you were going to cut me."

" Don't be silly, Spragge," said Tinker in a deep, sensible voice ; " but if one spoke to every Springfielder one met in the street one would never get anywhere. It can't be done."

" Isn't Evelyn looking *bad* ? " said Elizabeth, as they walked up St. Giles'. " You wouldn't believe it, but she used to look so nice at school." They didn't.

Making Conversation

As they went in to lunch, a genuinely middle-aged woman came up to Martha and said, " Excuse me a moment, Miss Freke." She looked so much like a schoolmistress that she gave Martha a dentist-feeling in her stomach.

" Excuse me. I heard that you had not joined the S.C.F., and I thought there might be certain aspects of it you might find objectionable. Do you feel like joining the G.S.M. ? "

" Thank you very much. What is that ? "

" It is the Guild of St. Margaret. We have meetings and discussions with Canon Runciman. It is smaller and more——"

As the schoolmistress faltered, Martha too felt the embarrassment to which the English are prone at the mention of religion. They stood and mouthed at each other.

" More spiritual in tone," said the woman at last, and was glad to turn away before getting an answer.

Mr. Bickersteth's lectures on Cicero were on Mondays, Wednesdays and Fridays in the hall of Wimshurst College. He

Making Conversation

had sent his son to Winchester and had not educated his daughter; but he liked to have women students at his lectures because they laughed at his jokes. The women sat apart from the men, four from Springfield, four from St. Dymphna's Hall, two from St. Tubno's and two from St. Ethelburga's. Martha and Helen and Elizabeth had their noses well powdered, and were equipped with new note-books and fountain-pens. There was an old man with grey hair taking notes, but most of them looked very young and spotty, except one who had only one arm and two who were lame.

" What a lot of growths," said Helen on the way back.

" There was a rather nice one with a red face in the corner," said Elizabeth.

That first Monday evening they had a class with Mr. Barrington-Ramsbotham, on Greek Unseens and grammar. He paced the room like a caged beast, and avoided their eyes. When he tried to balance himself on the fender and failed, they giggled.

" I am afraid," he said, " that the purity

Making Conversation

of my Greek has been violated by excessive reading of Polybius." Then he went to the blackboard and said, " I hope you will be able to understand my cursive script." He gave them a lecture on poetic diction. " Not *you*, but *thou*, when you are translating poetry. Not ' old age.' There is a far better word, which is ' *eld.*' Eld. Eld. And this poetic epithet for Hephaistos—I suggest ' the *storied cripple.*' No, Miss Parker, we cannot permit ' the toiling and perspiring farmer ' ; we must find something better."

" Sweating," said Helen.

" No, not sweating. I suggest *moiling* : ' the husbandman, toiling and moiling.' "

On Wednesdays they went to him separately with Latin prose. As Martha climbed the staircase, she heard Mr. Barrington-Ramsbotham say very distinctly to the scout, " And if Lord Pottinger rings up, tell him I'm busy." The social aspect of her tutor was something new ; and then he said, " I think Sir Randolph Blennerhassett is a relation of yours. He was very kind to me in Salonika." It was incredible

Making Conversation

that anyone could be important enough to be able to be kind to Mr. Ramsbotham. But he was much nicer alone, and regarded her prose sympathetically.

" That is a picturesque phrase, but I'm afraid it won't do."

" Oh, but I found it in Pliny."

" If Pliny wrote that, Miss Freke, he was a bold, bad man."

In the hushed and reverent atmosphere of a tutorial, this seemed a good joke. " These are my suggestions," he said, and read aloud his fair copy with an affected nonchalance which was overpowering.

" Yes," said Martha, " but I don't quite see that quotation."

" That," he said, with a slight smirk, " I put in out of sheer wantonness."

At the end he said, " You live near Adderbury, don't you ? "

" Yes, I live at Coombe."

" Coombe. Do you know the Pilkingthorpes ? "

" No, I'm afraid not."

"Or the Smith-Coffins of Dundersbury ? "

Making Conversation

"No, that's in the other direction beyond Adderbury."

"That's extraordinary," he said, "because I know that county. And that part of the county too. But I don't know Coombe. In fact, I didn't know there was anyone living at Coombe."

"I think the Ram's much nicer alone," said Elizabeth one evening after dinner, as she lay voluptuously on Martha's bed and kicked the cushions.

"So do I," said Martha.

"Darling, you're not falling in love with him, too?"

"Of course not."

"Wouldn't it be marvellous to have someone hopelessly in love with one?"

"Oh, I don't know."

"Wouldn't it be heavenly," said Helen, "to lead a life of luxury, instead of being shut up here with all these smelly women?"

"I don't want to be anyone's mistress," said Martha. "I'm not fond enough of physical exercise."

"But wouldn't it be nice to have someone

Making Conversation

sending one orchids? And taking one out to lunch in a car?" said Helen.

"That couldn't happen here, because of the chaperon rules."

"But as we don't know anyone, the chaperon rules don't make any difference."

"Perhaps there will be more men now the war is over."

"I've just had a prize of £10 from St. Mungo's for Latin prose," said Elizabeth. "I think I'll buy some new hats." Her ears were now well covered with her hair, which was dark and marcel-waved, and she had discarded most of the underclothes with which she had come up.

"I suppose you'll get one with a rose behind your ear, and think you're Carmen," said Helen. She had red hair and a pale face with high cheek-bones. "But it would be much more sense to get some really transparent silk stockings. Those look like wool."

"They're not; they're specially heavy silk that mummy always gets."

"Of course she would. And you both

Making Conversation

must take the sleeves out of your evening dresses, and most of the backs."

" Oh, but I couldn't possibly ! " said Martha.

" Don't be silly ! And I'll take you to the chemist and get you the necessary toilet preparations."

There was a knock at the door, and Miss Tinker put her head round it. " Excuse me, Freke," she said. " I wonder if you would mind making a little less noise. It's getting late, and Hutchinson has a touch of 'flu " ; and she shut the door very quietly.

" I'm going to stay up all night," said Elizabeth. So they clattered out and went to her room, where they made coffee and read aloud to each other from Russian novels and the *Nation and Athenæum*. When dawn broke, they had burned all their coal ; their eyelids were swollen and the powder had congealed on their noses ; and they went to bed and missed breakfast and the morning's lectures.

The next evening there was a notice on Miss Legge's door across the passage, saying, " Private. Please do not disturb."

" So she's ill, too," said Martha.

" It must be that skin-disease of hers," said Helen. " She's trying to treat it at home."

But as they went to the pantry to boil a kettle, they heard a buzz of voices behind the same door, and concluded she was having a deathbed scene. Some chords were struck on a piano, and women's voices began to sing a hymn.

" It's something very esoteric," said Martha.

" It sounds Low Church," said Elizabeth.

" Let's listen," said Helen.

After the " Amen," someone began to speak in a subdued tone, and they were afraid they wouldn't hear, until a louder phrase occurred—" Healthy minds in healthy bodies." They dared not breathe, and as they huddled together near the keyhole, they had pins and needles in their limbs. They thought they heard the words " decadent and exotic " ; and there was no

Making Conversation

doubt about the climax, " show them the error of their ways, and the grace of corporate spirit ; Amen." Then the conversation seemed to drop to a lower plane, and they heard a voice, which might be Miss Parker's, saying, " After all, the only thing that matters is service." Another voice said, " Look at me ! I'm C. of E., but my grandfather is an atheist, my father is an agnostic, and my mother is a mere lover of pleasure." Someone else muttered, among other things, " A not very practising orthodox Anglican. What William James calls the religion of healthy-mindedness." And a louder voice said, " We must evangelise, not only the J.C.R.s, but the S.C.R.s." Then someone began to read a paper, which seemed to be about the struggle for existence in the animal world, mentioning " Nature red in tooth and claw." It was rather dull, and Martha and Helen and Elizabeth went back to the pantry, where they shouted with laughter for some time.

CHAPTER XII

AT the beginning of the next term a letter arrived from Miss Macdonald, saying, " The first-year students for Honour Moderations will attend Miss Craigie's class on Thucydides in St. Dymphna's Hall, and I hope this is the last I shall hear on the subject."

" I love Thucydides," said Miss Parker, with a far-away look in her eyes.

" What an unnatural passion, Gladys," said Helen. They called her Gladys now.

" But darling Ramsbotham is lecturing on Pindar," said Elizabeth. " We *must* go. Fancy going to a class in a stuffy woman's college. It's too much like school."

" And it's at nine o'clock in the morning, too."

" Hell," said Elizabeth. " Let's go round and tell the Ramsbotham."

Gladys, who had been sitting on the floor, got up slowly, first on one knee and

Making Conversation

then the other, and flounced out. The others put on their best clothes, and went immediately after a college lunch. As they climbed the dark staircase at St. Jude's, they clutched each other's hands. A gramophone was playing, and there was a scout on the landing, who said Mr. Barrington-Ramsbotham had a lunch-party.

" Oh, but it's very urgent," said Elizabeth. " Will you tell him some students from Springfield want to see him at once ? "

Through the half-open door they heard someone say, " Oh, my God ! " and it was Mr. Barrington-Ramsbotham. As he came out, with a few crumbs on his waistcoat, there was a combined smell of incense, cigarette-smoke, coffee and brandy ; and behind him there was a dim, panelled room populated with young men.

" Please, Mr. Ramsbotham," said Elizabeth in a childish voice, " we do so want to come to your Pindar lectures."

" Really ? And what is there to stop you ? " he asked in a tone that was sharper and less rich than usual.

Making Conversation

" Miss Macdonald won't let us, and she wants us to do Thucydides instead."

" In that case," he said, " far be it from me to interfere with the discipline of your college."

" But we do so want to come to your lectures."

He could not control a smirk, and said, " If you would care to attend, as a matter of general interest, I shall always be glad to see you."

They began to say thank you, but he went on, " I may remind you that my lectures are at eleven o'clock, and *not* at two in the afternoon."

" Is that one of the new Ravel records ? ' asked Elizabeth.

" Yes," he said. " Now you must excuse me "; and he went back and slammed the door.

" That man is a toad," said Helen, " and I'm not going near his damned lectures."

" What a lovely time men have compared with women," said Elizabeth. " Lovely sitting-rooms and bedrooms and

Making Conversation

lunch-parties. They can enjoy themselves without women, but women can't enjoy themselves without men."

" What about Sappho ? " said Helen.

" I don't believe it," said Elizabeth.

" Professor Herbert Worry," said Martha, " says she probably didn't mean it, and was only copying poetry written by men."

" Have you heard about Bagshaw ? " said Helen. Bagshaw was a fourth-year medical student.

" Yes, Evelyn told me," said Elizabeth. " They say that Hogg types all her lecture-notes for her, although she's a second-year doing French. She does all Bagshaw's cooking and washing-up too, and they never come into Hall, but you could hardly blame them for that. It doesn't prove anything."

Anyway, they never felt the same again about Mr. Barrington-Ramsbotham ; and Elizabeth began to cut her tutorials " Darling, you will have to go half an hour earlier ; I'm going to cut him," she would

Making Conversation

say. So Martha had to explain: " Miss Spragge is very sorry, she has to meet an old friend who is passing through Oxford by train," or " Miss Spragge is very sorry; she has a bad cold and has quite lost her voice."

They came back for the Summer Term with a lot of new clothes, and Elizabeth had most, as she was the richest of them. One evening, Helen and Martha found her quivering after an interview with Evelyn Tinker. " Evelyn says it isn't good form to wear summer dresses to lectures. She says one ought to wear a neatly tailored shirt and a tweed skirt, because it looks more workmanlike."

" Tell her to mind her own business," said Helen.

" She said she didn't like the tulle hats we have, and that they didn't look like ladies."

" Tell her to go to Hell."

Elizabeth burst into tears and said, " She said if I went on like this, I should end up on the streets. And I told her I didn't care, and that I couldn't imagine anything more perfectly thrilling!"

They gave her some coffee and cigarettes and lemon-squash, and she powdered her face; and after that they drank coffee and lemon-squash alternately until they had finished the bottle.

"Evelyn says that the way I wear my clothes is a provocation to men, but I hadn't thought of it. And she says the chaperon rules are made to protect us against ourselves. She was trying to be very nice and sympathetic. And she says it's silly to carry a sunshade."

"I suppose it's better to burn one's face into blisters. But Orientals have sunshades and fans, even the men," said Martha.

"Oh, darling, what an idea!" said Elizabeth. "I must buy a fan."

So they all bought fans, and took them to Mr. Mott's lecture on the *Georgics* of Virgil. Some of the undergraduates sniggered. There were many more of them this term; Martha had a cousin up, called Tommy Blennerhassett, whom she

Making Conversation

remembered as a Boy Scout; she doubted if he would be interesting. And Elizabeth had two cousins, who asked her out to dine with their mother. That day she had a shampoo, marcel-wave, manicure and face-massage, and also a long bath before dinner. She came back on the stroke of eleven o'clock, which was when the gates were shut, and found Martha and Helen waiting anxiously in her room. " Well, what were they like ? " they asked.

She sat still and played with a necklace she had borrowed from Helen, although she had plenty of her own.

" *What were they like?* "

" Oh, they were rather sweet." And after a pause, she said, " I think they quite liked me." She said nothing further, and the tension grew until they said good night.

A surprising thing occurred in Springfield College. People were heard to say, " Do you know we're going to have a dance ? "

" Nonsense ! You mean just dancing together on Saturday nights."

Making Conversation

"No, a real dance, with real men, from eight to twelve."

"Can you dance?"

"Do you know any men?"

"Haven't some people got some brothers?"

It was true that some men as well as tutors had been seen recently in the college. Students were allowed to give them tea in public sitting-rooms, "if names were entered in a book provided for that purpose." Students who did not know these men averted their eyes when they met them in the front hall; and the men averted their eyes from the students. Now girls with brothers became increasingly popular. Elizabeth invited both her cousins to the dance, and Martha invited Tommy, who accepted in an unintelligent handwriting on pinkish notepaper. "I must apologise," he wrote, "for this rather aneamic" (the spelling was his) "looking paper; it is some I got in France, where tastes seem to run to pinks, mauves, etc. I haven't thanked you yet for the invitation. It is

Making Conversation

most noble of you to have thought of it, and the reference to my beautiful dancing as a child is sufficiently elusive to appear almost sarcastic. Cheerio!" Martha blushed to read it.

On the evening of the dance there was intense competition for the bathrooms. Martha emptied half a bottle of verbena crystals into her bath, which brought out a rash on her body. She was in tears as she dressed, and found she had spots on her forehead. She did not go into Hall for dinner, but gave Helen and Elizabeth boiled eggs and coffee in her room. They had a visit from Nita Rubinstein, an American Jewess who was spending a year at Oxford to get the atmosphere. She showed them her dress, and wailed, " I ordered it in Nile green and she's sent it in jade green! The model was in black, but I never wear black, it's too old for me." They tried not to look incredulous, as her figure was a mature one.

" I'd sell this cheap. It's a genuine Lanvin model, but I'd let it go for nothing,

Making Conversation

I feel so sick. I'd let it go for £20!"

There were no offers; and she asked, "Do you think it looks terrible in the bodice?"

"What you want," said Helen, "is something underneath. Have you never heard of a bust-bodice?"

"Oh, you could never go into a shop and ask for a thing like that, could you?" asked Nita, who was shocked.

Some of the students were transformed as if by a miracle. Miss Stubbs was in tomato-coloured chiffon with lips to match. Evelyn Tinker had a blue ribbon round her head. But one of the Titmusses from Holmlea had the sleeves of an under-garment showing under white tulle, and the president of the J.C.R. took her into the cloak-room with some safety-pins.

Martha recognised Tommy by his large forehead, which was altogether out of proportion to his intellect. He now had a small moustache. She thanked him for coming, and he said it was jolly good of her to ask him. She introduced him to her friends,

Making Conversation

and then quite wildly to everyone who stood around, including Gladys Parker. Martha and Tommy had the first dance together, and she stepped on his feet.

" What school are you reading ? " she asked him.

" Agriculture," he said. " For my sins."

" I didn't know there was a school of agriculture."

" There isn't, it's a diploma. As a matter of fact, we spend most of our time at Reading, wandering about over Suttons' Seeds."

Some more men were introduced to her, and she found herself dancing with one whose face seemed familiar. " I've seen you at Bickersteth's lectures," he said; and he was the red-faced man they had noticed.

" I adore Mr. Bickersteth," said Martha. " I love his jokes about mullets. When he had influenza, we wanted to go and leave him some flowers and grapes, but we didn't dare."

Then her feet were badly tied up and

Making Conversation

she apologised. " Perhaps it would be better," said the man, " if we didn't talk so much."

They revolved in silence, until the same thing happened again, and worse. " Perhaps it would be better to talk, after all," said the man, " and then you won't think so much about your feet."

So they talked about college and the chaperon rules, and the dons who were sitting on the daïs, from which the High Table had been removed. " ' Dons on the daïs serene '—Henry Newbolt," said the man facetiously.

" I'm afraid I can't stand Henry Newbolt," said Martha.

" Nor can I," said the man. She was surprised and relieved, and felt they had established a contact.

There were several dances for which she had no partner, and she retired to her room to hide her shame. She found people sitting out on the stairs. It was hardly possible ; but on the top of the kitchen stairs there was someone being embraced, who looked like a high official of the Christian Fellowship.

At the end of the last dance, Tommy stiffened to attention for " God save the King," and then said, " Could you come to tea one day ? "

" Thank you awfully ! I would love to."

" Look here, would you have to bring a shap ? " (Short for chaperon.)

Martha said boldly, " No, I won't. Can I bring another girl ? "

" That will be topping. There's an awfully nice man on my staircase, and I'll ask him."

" Well, I'll bring an awfully nice girl."

That night she said to Helen, " Will you come out to tea with me and be awfully stupid ? "

Some first-years were discussing the dance. " Way back home," said Miss Rubinstein, " I'd have been kissed after every dance. And to-night I've only been kissed three times. Life seems all wrong somehow. I don't think any of you girls have come alive." The others looked

Making Conversation

conscious of never having been kissed. " Of course," she went on, " some girls come alive sooner than others. It's a funny thing, but the man who made me come alive was one who was introduced to me by my own family." They looked polite and attentive. " And there's a boy who writes letters to me now who's afraid I'll fall for an English boy. Sidney his name is. ' Nita,' he says, ' never forget we were born under the shadow of the stars and stripes.' "

" Did you see Tompkinson ? " asked someone else.

" Yes, isn't she *deep* ? "

Martha and Helen felt a thrill of law-breaking when they went to tea with Tommy in one of the smaller colleges.

" I'm awfully sorry," said Tommy, " but the man I was telling you about had to go and play tennis. However, I've got another man from across the quad."

" I'm sure he's awfully nice too," said Helen.

The door opened, and in came the

Making Conversation

red-faced man from Bickersteth's lectures. His name was Henry Butts.

"As a matter of fact," said Tommy slowly, "this college is rather divided into the athletic section and the other fellows. I mean the literary crowd. Mr. Butts is one of the latter."

This was an unexpected element in the tea-party, and it was not what they had hoped. Helen settled down with Tommy and the chocolate cakes, and smiled brilliantly and said, "How topping!" at intervals; while Martha relapsed into her usual style with Mr. Butts.

"I am not really a literary person," he said; "I think I am an average man."

"I can't believe it," she said. "That would be so boring."

"Why? Have you met so many of them?"

"No, I don't think I've ever met one. All my friends are abnormal."

"Then it ought to be quite an experience for you."

"I don't know. It's so hard to recognise

Making Conversation

the normal. Don't psycho-analysts say that everyone is abnormal in one way or another?"

"Do they?"

"Or perhaps that's because Freud only has lunatics to practise on."

"Perhaps."

"Of course, one never met any normal people during the war. Were you in the Army?"

"Yes," said Mr. Butts.

"I was entirely against the war," said Martha.

"So was I," said Mr. Butts. He had an amiable smile and a pleasant, slightly porcine face.

The party went on until 6 o'clock, and on the way out they looked for spies in the shape of women dons and third-years. The next morning they saw Mr. Butts in the *Georgics* lecture and bowed. There was a rule, but it was no longer enforced, against women students communicating with undergraduates at lectures, " even though they had private relations with

Making Conversation

them." The next time, after a lecture on the *Poetics* of Aristotle, they introduced him to Elizabeth, and he asked them to have coffee at the Cadena with two of his friends. There they sat at a marble-topped table, in a greenish yellow light which made them all look jaundiced, and they ate buns.

" Oxford is several centuries out of date," said one of the young men, whose name was Isaacs. " I object to the monastic system. I'm hoping to have a motion about it in the Union next term."

Tinker and Porter came in, and averted their eyes. Elizabeth was telling Mr. Butts in a low voice about the cruelty of Barrington-Ramsbotham. " He lets me knock at the door for several minutes, when he knows perfectly well I'm there. And last night he told me my prose was an *autoschediasmos*, and I hadn't any idea what it meant. He just does it to show off."

" What we want," said the other young man, " is a social club for progressive people."

Elizabeth began to attend lectures with

Making Conversation

greater regularity. But it was no use. One day she walked into lunch, with her largest tulle hat and waving a fan, and announced, " I've been sent down."

A crowd gathered. " Oh, *Spragge* ! " breathed Tinker, who had come over from the second-year table. " What for ? " asked several people at once.

" Because I was keeping out a better woman. And you needn't call me *Spragge*, when you're supposed to be a friend of mine, and I know you aren't. And that creature Ramsbotham went and said I had been a severe trial to him, and had committed a grave breach of etiquette and discipline calling on an unmarried tutor in his rooms."

" But there were three of us," said Martha.

" He wasn't in any danger," said Helen.

They took Elizabeth out and gave her lunch in the Cadena, in an atmosphere of unrelieved gloom. " You needn't feel guilty about me," she said ; " it will be your turn next."

CHAPTER XIII

NEXT term Martha and Helen came up meaning to work. But the first thing Martha found in her pigeon-hole was an invitation for them both to lunch with Tommy. So they put on their new navy-blue costumes and staggered off on their highest heels.

"I'm so glad you're beginning to have heels on your shoes at last, dear," said Helen.

Henry Butts was there, in very long plus-fours, which made them wonder if tweeds might not be right after all, as Tinker had said. Lunch began with prawn salad and went on with chicken; the rolls were a little stale, but it was better than Springfield; and they had some tepid white wine.

"Let's turn down a glass for Miss Spragge," said Henry. "She's a martyr to antediluvianism."

Making Conversation

"Look here," said Tommy, "I think it's jolly sporting of you girls to stick it. I don't see how you can stay here at all, when you might be having a good time in London or somewhere. I really don't."

Helen kicked Martha and checked her from saying anything highbrow. "Well, we've got to stay here," she explained carefully, in words of one syllable, "because we're too poor to have a good time, and we have to earn our livings afterwards."

"How perfectly rotten," said Tommy. "I know a lot of girls have to nowadays." He was deeply sympathetic, and almost in tears.

Helen was talking to Henry about the verse translations of Professor Herbert Worry, and Martha overheard as much as possible. After lunch they put on the gramophone and danced.

"You know I can't," said Martha to Henry.

"Nonsense," he said. "All you want is practice. Now one, *two*, one, *two*."

The next time they saw him at a lecture,

Making Conversation

they went to the Cadena again; and soon they went to the Cadena without going to lectures. By an unwritten and unspoken agreement, Henry was to be found in Cornmarket Street at about eleven o'clock, and they always pretended to be surprised.

Then he asked them to tea. He had a nondescript room hung with etchings, which might be good, and his friends appeared to be neither athletes nor æsthetes. They smoked pipes and knocked them out on the window-sill. " Hopkins ! " said one. " Conscious artistry ! " and it seemed they were talking about poetry. One of them read a regional poem about Essex which sounded familiar, but Martha and Helen were out of their depth. They did not know if it was his own or by a well-known Georgian poet. Another read a war-poem, which faded off into regional in the end. Someone mentioned the O.U.D.S., and said, " I think it ought to be a good show. At any rate, it will be very good for the club. It brings people together." There were murmurs of assent.

Making Conversation

"I myself," said Mr. Isaacs, "feel strongly about the Union. It is one of the institutions which matter most in post-war Oxford. It has traditions to be carried on; and I don't know if you feel the same as I do, but I feel they're not safe in the hands of Gordon. Hang it all, the fellow's a Jew!"

"Yes, and what about the Angles?" said a small, dark man called Samuelson. "I consider it a disgrace that there should be clubs for the Scotch, the Welsh, the Irish, the Americans, and even the Indians, and nothing for the genuine English. My appeal has not met with the support I expected; I have had no answer from Belloc or Chesterton."

"I am writing an article for the *Mercury*," said someone with a moustache and spectacles; "at least, I have reason to believe they'll take it, and it's too long for any other paper. On an English Renaissance. Something on the lines of the Irish literary movement, supported by dancing, music and craftwork. There's Grubb, for

Making Conversation

instance. He's deeply identified with the soil."

"Goodness, but that man's good," said Henry. "Did you see that 'Nocturne' in the *Observer* last Sunday?"

"Did you hear about Devlin?" asked someone.

"Hush, John," said someone else; "there are ladies present!"

"I don't think it matters," said Henry. "Devlin," he explained, "is a peculiarly unpleasant type of Irishman. He was relieved of a portion of his garments by some people in college last night. In other words, he was de-bagged. It may do him good."

"Geographical impossibility," said someone, referring to Ireland.

"Hang it all," said Isaacs, "one may not agree with the method, but it's pretty hard for fellows who've been at the war to come back and find these fellows who haven't behaving like this. There are limits."

"It is particularly embarrassing," said

Making Conversation

Samuelson, " when one of one's friends, whom one has always considered as a friend, behaves in a manner for which one can find no justification. One would like to, but one can't. I feel deeply about friendship. I have prided myself on an almost Elizabethan conception of friendship. There are certain old and very precious things "—here he knocked out his pipe—" which the world has come to neglect, and which I have come to appreciate. Among them is loyalty."

" That's all right, old chap," said Isaacs. "We know how you feel about it." As the conversation grew personal, someone showed Martha and Helen some photographs of El Greco pictures, and said, " These are on the verge of becoming odiously affected, don't you think ? " They were so impressed that on the way home they hardly giggled.

Oxford was carpeted again in autumn leaves; and Henry at a *Poetics* lecture suggested a walk in the country. Martha and Helen discussed it after dinner. " I

Making Conversation

don't like walking," said Helen, " and the country doesn't suit my type. It makes my face shine."

" I should be afraid," said Martha, " that one's conversation would run out."

" There's no fear of that with you, my dear."

" I don't know. I always talk too much or too little."

" That's because you worry too much. And you haven't any idea of reciprocity. The English haven't."

" Cat ! " said Martha, and met Henry at 2 o'clock the next day at Carfax. She wore thick shoes and her usual coat and skirt, with a yellow woollen jumper instead of a shirt blouse. Jumpers were just coming in. They took a 'bus down St. Aldate's and the Abingdon Road, past the gasworks, and she enjoyed having her fare paid, though it was only twopence. At that moment the good college women from Springfield were setting off on their bicycles, some to play hockey, and others to gather berries which they would arrange in jars from Liberty's.

Making Conversation

On the seat in front of them sat an undergraduate, without a hat and in tweeds like Henry, with a beautiful girl who might be a manicurist having a half-holiday; and Martha felt much more sympathetic to her than to Tinker and Porter.

They got out and walked towards Hinksey Hill. "Do you know your Arnold?" asked Henry.

"*Essays in Criticism*," said Martha, "but I'm not awfully fond of his verse."

"There's good stuff in it all the same. Do you mind if I light a pipe?"

She did not. It reminded her of the advertisements "Be a man and smoke a pipe." To go out with a man who smoked a pipe seemed to be a more striking breach of the chaperon rules than to go out with one who did not. And none of her mother's friends had pipes. But unfortunately he found great difficulty in lighting it.

They discussed the poetry written by critics, and the criticism written by poets. Wordsworth and Coleridge; poems and ballads; *Kubla Khan*; dope; De Quincey;

Making Conversation

Beckford. Then they said simultaneously, " Ernest Dowson ! " Henry quoted " I have been faithful to thee, Cynara, in my fashion " ; and Martha said, " Do you know that little one at the beginning, ' They are not long, the weeping and the laughter, love and desire and hate ' ? " He did. They agreed that Arthur Symons had written a beautiful introduction. So they came to the Symbolists ; Mallarmé ; Rimbaud and the colours of vowels, and that lovely portrait of him by Fantin-Latour. There was a line in Baudelaire about someone's voice being perfume and her breath being music. (Did Henry know it ? No, he didn't, for once.) Poor Baudelaire. Poor Gérard de Nerval. Poor Villiers de l'Isle Adam. What about Albert Samain ? " *Mon âme est une Enfante en robes de parade.*" Henry didn't know it—one up to Martha.

They left the road and walked along a narrow, muddy path. Henry thought he had better go in front because he knew the way ; and Martha noticed from behind how large and red his ears were. They did

Making Conversation

not strike her as repulsive, but as interesting and characteristic; though his mother should have tied them down when he was a child. Had he a mother? Undoubtedly, and very likely a dull one. He stopped several times to re-light his pipe. Then they found themselves on the brow of a hill overlooking Oxford; he spread the mackintosh he had been carrying, and they sat on it.

Henry put on a pair of tortoiseshell rims to look at the view, while Martha powdered her nose. She was very hot from hurrying along behind him, and sometimes taking three steps to his two.

" You are an introvert," he said.

" Oh, no, really ? "

" While I am looking at the view, you are only thinking of how you look."

" Don't you think," she said, " those distinctions are bound to be very relative ? "

She was preparing to enjoy a discussion about herself, when they saw a strange group of figures in the lane. They were small men in top-hats and frock-coats, and

Making Conversation

as they came nearer, it was evident they were Japanese. They stopped a few yards away, talking a foreign language, and began to point. Martha and Henry noticed for the first time that they were sitting under a small, bare tree; and they heard certain sounds recurring, which were " Skoll-ah Jipp-see, Skoll-ah Jipp-see, Matt-yew Ah-nol." So they concluded it was the Matthew Arnold country, and arose in shame and went away.

They had tea in a public house. A foxy-faced woman made an offer of a " private room," from which they recoiled. The public room was decorated with a large stuffed fish in a glass case; a photograph of the publican holding a giant vegetable-marrow; ash-trays recommending Worthingtons'; and the coloured advertisement of an insurance company, which showed a married couple enjoying a respected and comfortable old age. There was a smell of stale drinks, the tea was black and stewed, and the butter was margarine. The cakes had been made of " Cakiflor " and were

Making Conversation

served in paper cases presented free with the packet. But Martha reflected that it was only at a women's tea-party that the food had to be good ; at a mixed party it didn't matter.

It was getting dark as they came out ; and they started when a figure materialised in the shadows and asked for some cigarettes. It was an old man, and Henry gave him some Gold Flake. The public house had not been the legendary English inn ; but this might be a genuine English rustic for the English Renaissance.

" Thank you, sir," he said. " It takes a real gentleman to give a poor man a cigarette. Or a real lady. Now, the ladies that drove the motors when the war was on, they'd always give you a smoke, if it was only a Woodbine. Real ladies. No matter what bloody things was said about them." Henry and Martha quickened their pace, but the shadow accompanied them. " Times has changed. There's the vicar into Bablockleigh, he does measure his land with a false rood-measure. But I'm not fooled.

Making Conversation

The doctor into Bablockleigh, he says I'm not right in the head. But I do often stay awake of a night working out the cube roots to many places of decimals." Henry took Martha's arm, and she tried to keep in step with him. " Could you tell me, sir," asked the shadow, " how many gallons of water——" But at that minute they heard a long-distance 'bus behind them, and stopped it.

The next morning at lectures, Martha hardly looked at Henry ; it was delightful to think she had a " private relation " with an undergraduate, and that no one knew. She did not suppose she was in love with him. " You haven't ever been in love, have you ? " she asked Helen.

" No. Only with Cousin Dickie after he was killed in the war. Not before."

" That's necrophily, dear. But I'm sure if one were, there would be no doubt about it. Like a revelation or a conversion."

" Even if one were in love with an undergraduate, one could hardly marry him."

" No. It would be rather fun to live with

him for a bit, but the chaperon rules would get in the way."

"Of course, one could get married and go down."

"Yes, but then one might have to have children, and I think I would rather do Greats than have a child."

The next time, however, that Martha was hurrying to a tutorial, with a barely finished Latin prose, she was surprised to see Helen and Henry together outside the West Gate tea-rooms. They were absorbed in conversation, and she felt a distinct twinge of jealousy. Helen was double-crossing her. There was no doubt about jealousy as an emotion, it was more unmistakable than love.

But Helen cut Henry's next tea-party, and Martha was there alone. They discussed an Oxford magazine called the *New Dryad*, and decided that it wouldn't last long. She was saying that the editor's teeth were grey, and that some people said it was a sign of addiction to laudanum, when she had a queer feeling in her back.

Making Conversation

After a few seconds she realised it was Henry's hand, but went on talking more than ever. The poem by Miss Mackerel of St. Tubno's, she said, had a distinct Lesbian tendency. Henry might not believe it, but Miss Bagshaw was heard to have said she didn't like the summer, because it stopped her wearing a man's overcoat. And some people said she grew livid with passion at the sight of a camisole in a shop-window.

Then his arm came around her waist, and she went quite limp and waited for something to happen. He kissed her tentatively, and she began to giggle. He drew back and said, " What's the matter ? "

" Oh, nothing," she said, and shook with laughter, without quite knowing why.

" Do you mind ? "

" Oh, not at all, if it gives you any pleasure. But I may as well tell you it doesn't mean anything to me."

" So that's how you feel, is it ? " he said, standing with his back to the fireplace, while she lay in a heap in the chair. They were both blushing. " All right, I won't."

" I'm so sorry, but it seemed so funny, just as we were talking about that magazine. It didn't seem to lead up to it."

" I see."

" It might have been all right at some other time. Did you ever want to kiss me before ? "

" Yes. That day when we were interrupted by the Japanese."

" Oh, fancy ! I wish you had."

" I'm sorry," he said, " that I haven't enough experience to make love to you in the way you appreciate. I couldn't make you out. Sometimes I thought you were too damned sophisticated, and sometimes I thought not. Now I know."

Martha sat up and said, " You don't imagine I've been kissed such a lot before, do you ? "

" Well, what else am I to think ? You said yourself——"

" I did not ! But if that's what you think, I'm going home, anyway. Good-bye."

He held out her coat with the air of a

Making Conversation

shop-assistant who displays mourning to the bereaved customer.

"How did it go off?" asked Helen that evening.

"Very badly, darling. It side-slipped completely. But I don't care. He has such hideous ears."

The next time she saw Henry at a lecture he avoided her eye, and she felt like a woman with a past.

CHAPTER XIV

NEXT term, Henry did not go to any lectures, but worked hard for Mods, and went down with a war degree. Martha and Helen and Gladys did papers on Virgil for Mr. Mott, and tried to get up the subject of Roman agriculture. One Sunday afternoon, Mrs. Mott asked them to tea in North Oxford, and Gladys set off on a bicycle, while Martha and Helen walked painfully up the Banbury Road on high heels, with their faces well made-up. The party started at 4 o'clock, with a conversation on lawn-mowers. There were four undergraduates of the serious student type, who called Mr. Mott " sir " and handed bread-and-butter ; and there was Miss Œnone Mott, who said, " I do think it's noble of you girls to go to daddy's lectures. I couldn't stick going to college."

" Nowadays," said Mrs. Mott, " it's quite the thing for girls to take up something. Œnone's very keen on amateur theatricals. Last year she took up folk-dancing, and this year she's taking up the ballet."

"Oh, Mr. Simpson," said Œnone to one of the serious students, "you really ought to join our ballet-class, because you're small and light. You would love it."

Mr. Simpson's greyish face turned red, as he did not like to be reminded that he was small. Martha noticed he was not so ugly as the others, and that he had curly hair and perfect ears.

"I hear," said Mrs. Mott, "that Zara McCullough, the actress, is coming to live in Oxford."

"Isn't it thrilling?" said Œnone.

"But I shall not call," said Mrs. Mott.

"Ah, my dear," said her husband, "we have nothing against actresses as such. Times have changed, and actresses are very useful in a place. Look at the help they give in amateur theatricals. Madame Riposo helps the boys at Bellevue every year with their Gilbert and Sullivan."

"They may be very well in their way,"

Making Conversation

said Mrs. Mott, " and I should speak to her if she was introduced at theatricals, but that is not the same thing as receiving her."

Œnone produced a small lacquer box from a drawer, and Helen said to one of the young men, " Splendid ! I'm dying for a cigarette."

But it was opened to display a brilliantly enamelled star and a red and yellow ribbon.

" This is the decoration," said Mrs. Mott, " that the Sultan of Ponga gave Mr. Mott as a token of regard. You know the heir apparent was one of his pupils."

" Yes," said Mr. Mott, " and a very gentlemanly young fellow he was, to be sure."

It was ten minutes to five, and the guests began to go. " Good-bye," said the Motts ; " come and see us again next term."

Simpson walked back with Martha and Helen. " You wouldn't guess," he said, " that Mott was one of the premier authorities in Europe on Latin prosody. With the possible exception of von Erfurt-Hermannsdorp, he is *the* authority."

Making Conversation

" What a deadly place this is," said Helen.

" I enjoy Oxford," said Simpson ; " it's an escape from life."

" I don't mind Oxford," said Martha, " but I don't like work."

" Work is an anodyne," he said.

He was sad but friendly as they said good-bye. They did not meet him at lectures, as he was a year ahead of them.

" Could we ask him to a college dance ? " asked Martha.

" He's a bit dreary," said Helen, " but it might be an anodyne for him. He's a bit small too, but he'd do for you."

" I think his head is rather Late Roman."

It was a shock of pleasure to Martha to find a note in her pigeon-hole in a small and scholarly handwriting, with the initials F. J. S. in the corner. Simpson had invited them to lunch, which was the nicest meal to go out to, because they were really hungry ; and there wasn't the agony of rushing back after dinner before the gate shut.

Making Conversation

There was another serious student there, and they drank claret, because some don had said that it was the drink of professional scholars. They ate a rather good steak, and felt warm and comfortable and discussed anodynes.

"There must be pleasanter ones than work," said Helen; "for instance, drink and dancing."

"And flirtation," said Simpson sadly; "but dancing is three parts flirtation."

"After that, I can hardly ask you to a Springfield dance," said Martha.

He seemed not to be listening and went on, "Dancing and flirtation and playing Rugger and working for Schools are all the same. They're all an escape from life, and an attempt to reconstruct life on a small scale, in a way in which we can hope to be more successful than in the real thing. All these worlds are microcosms, but not exactly. There is something false about all of them."

Helen was sleepy, after drinking port as well as claret. "It's odd," she said, and yawned, "how we spend so much time worrying about examinations, which are really things that don't exist at all. They're just imaginary. They're a figment."

"Do you know the only joke in Liddell and Scott?" asked the other man. They said no, and when he told it, remembered that they did. It was about the Greek word "sycophant," which might be derived from the word for fig, but "probably this was a figment."

"Oh, my God, what a joke!" said Helen, and fell into hysterical laughter. "What a perfect Oxford joke." The serious student looked a little hurt.

"There's the Springfield Boat Club," said Martha, "that's a microcosm, and a very nasty little microcosm too. So is college life, so-called; and all those clubs, with their executive committees, are microcosms inside them. But I don't agree about dancing being flirtation. It's art."

Having raised the whole problem of æsthetics, they went home and made tea.

Making Conversation

"It's very hard getting out of one microcosm into another," said Helen. "Going out to lunch puts one off Springfield for a whole day."

"It's drinking that does it," said Martha. "It creates a world of illusion, just like the Christian Fellowship."

"Not so bad as that. Unless you get D.T.s."

They didn't go to dinner in Hall, but had coffee and buns.

"I don't know if art is just another escape from life," said Martha. "Anyway, it's a better one than flirtation."

"One of those psycho-analysts," said Helen, "thinks that æsthetic appreciation is all sex."

"Do you mean that when Gladys chooses a tea-service with pink roses on it, it's the same as falling in love?"

"It's all relative, darling."

"Yes, but there must be a big gap somewhere. Do you know that Ernest Jones says Sappho was perfectly right about the physical symptoms of falling in love? You

Making Conversation

know that poem about your face going green, and your tongue sticking to the roof of your mouth, and your legs going like jelly?"

"Very likely."

"I believe I might be falling in love with Simpson."

"I wouldn't, if I were you."

"I wonder what his Christian name is."

"It begins with F., and he keeps it pretty dark. I expect it's Frederick. Freddy."

Simpson came to the college dance at the end of term, and Martha endured a moment of agony before dancing with him, which was like the dentist-feeling of her childhood. She also shook at the knees. But he was not hard to follow, though he danced beautifully. He was very graceful, and seemed to taper from a square curly head to small, pointed feet, like a Victorian caricature.

"Just imagine," he said, "if someone were to turn the light off now, and to tell all these couples to copulate on the spot,

Making Conversation

what would be the result in about a year's time?"

" Frightful, I should think."

" Yes, monstrous."

" Isn't life awful?"

" Yes, and what about death?"

" Of course. Imagine all these people in eighty years' time, whether they copulate or not. By the way, isn't it odd how athletes are either terribly handsome, which happens occasionally, or perfectly hideous? That man dancing with Miss Stubbs is a Rugger Blue."

Something went wrong with her feet when he went backwards, and wanted her to go forwards; and he remarked, " Women can't take the initiative, as Aristotle said." Then he said, " I think we ought to work ourselves into a state of physical excitement."

" All right. Is this flirtation?"

" Yes. There's something about flirtation in Bradley. I can't quite remember the passage. About dogs."

" We could go into the Roberts Library,"

said Martha. " We're not supposed to sit out there."

There was spring in the air as they went into the garden. The spring must be coming, because it was Lent, and some extreme pietists had renounced the dance for that reason.

" There are buds on the trees," said Martha.

" I prefer them bare," he said.

" Does the spring make you feel melancholy ? "

" Yes, the autumn is better."

They went into the dark library, put on the light and began to look for Bradley.

" No, it's not this one," said Simpson, feverishly turning the leaves. " Perhaps it's this one. Something about being controlled by reality."

He was talking more than she was, and she wished he would be quiet. The table was littered with note-books and blotting-paper, and some myopic woman-student had left a pair of spectacles, which she would probably come back to fetch.

Making Conversation

"Well, how shall we begin?" said Martha.

"We might begin by holding hands," said Simpson with his back to her.

"Yes, there's a good line of Aldous Huxley, about 'quietly sweating palm to palm.'"

"Then it must be subtly graded," he said. "We must have a *klimax erotos*. There is a poem about it in the *Corpus*. I don't know if I could find it. It starts with that idea, and goes on with a mass of disgusting detail of a kind which is irrelevant to us."

"Never mind," said Martha. "It's getting late, and there isn't a *Corpus* here."

So he turned off the light, and they sat on the floor in front of the empty fire-grate, holding hands. She was shivering with cold and excitement, and his hand was clammy, too. There was a faint light through the window from the sky.

Then he said, "This floor's very uncomfortable. I think I ought to sit on that chair, and you ought to sit on my knee."

Making Conversation

" Oh, no, I couldn't possibly ! "

" Why not ? "

" I should hurt you, of course. Have you ever done it before ? "

" No, but I believe it's always done."

They were on their knees facing each other. Now he had moved and she saw his white shirt-front in the chair. She was almost in tears, but prepared for anything ; and with the severest misgivings, she lowered herself upon him, and heard his shirt crackle. She was conscious of her weight, and felt as if she were sitting on a dead body. She found herself praying for something to happen. It did, because the band in the hall played " God Save the King."

By the time they joined the crowd, people were already saying good-bye. " Good night, and thanks awfully." " It has been topping." " Jolly good show." " Jolly good of you to come." " Thank you for a most enjoyable evening, Miss Higginbottom." And so on.

" Did he kiss you ? " asked Helen, as the gates were shut.

Making Conversation

" Yes," said Martha, and realised as she said it that it was a lie. She stayed awake a long time thinking about it. Why hadn't he kissed her ? It was because he had started fussing about Bradley and talking too much. He probably had melancholia. Or perhaps it was shell-shock. It would be a whole-time job to look after him, but it would be worth it. One might take him to Vienna, to be cured by Dr. Freud. Would he write to her in the vacation ? Of course he must. He didn't know her address, but the college would forward it.

Twice a day at Coombe she waited for the post, and twice a day she was disappointed. She looked up melancholia in the encyclopædia, and decided that, whether Simpson had it or not, she almost certainly had it herself. The only hope was that she had something else called " sane melancholy." In melancholia there were three stages, that followed each other, depression, elevation and lucid interval ; while in " sane melancholy " there were only two, which alternated, depression and

Making Conversation

cheerfulness, without any interval, so that it seemed less sane than the disease. But this was an old encyclopædia anyway. Her Mods result was a third class, which was bad. It was evident that the world of scholarship was not her world; and flirtation was not much more satisfactory.

Mrs. Freke had some Indian paying-guests now, surprisingly enough. " I wouldn't have done it years ago," she said, " but these are very high-caste."

" How do you know ? " said Martha.

" Of course I know. I always have a feeling about it. And it doesn't matter so much now I haven't a daughter growing up at home."

Still this mysterious connection between the colour-bar and sex. Both the Indians were called Mr. Lal, and were uncle and nephew; and they had perfect manners and limpid eyes. The nephew, who was older than the uncle, was writing a thesis on philosophy at Cambridge, and they had discussions in the evenings. " He's certainly very black," said Mrs. Freke, " but

Making Conversation

he's perfectly Aryan. You can see that. And he lives almost entirely on fruit. He's very easy to cater for."

She enjoyed discussions on the metaphysics of love.

"Love," said Mr. Lal, " is a great world-force. Whether it be love between parent and child, brother and sister, or husband and wife, it is the same force. Only the manifestation is different. And in love, as in everything, there is the action and the reaction, which is equal and opposite to it."

"Do you mean," asked Martha, " that love can't be all on one side ? That you can't have unrequited love ? "

"Exactly," said Mr. Lal.

"But isn't that contrary to all human experience ? "

"The romances of popular literature and of the cinema," he said, " are all false."

"But couldn't someone want to kiss you when you didn't want them to ? And vice versa ? "

"You would always have wanted it

Making Conversation

first," he said (ignoring the " vice versa " out of politeness, she hoped). "You are just as responsible as they are."

" In the East," said the other Mr. Lal, " there is no romance. Only devotion. Our pure national culture is attacked and debased by obscene foreign importations, by the cinema and jazz-dancing. But we remain faithful to our ideals, to the great ideal of the Buddha. We want to *be*, we only want to BE ! "

" I thought the Indians had rejected Buddha," said Martha.

" Be quiet, dear," said her mother. " You're only interrupting. Do tell us, Mr. Lal, about the telepathic message you had from your aunt in India."

Martha went to bed and thought about the falsehood of romance. The Indians had child-marriage, and that saved a lot of trouble.

One morning, Mrs. Freke read aloud from the newspaper, "' Double Gas-poisoning Death Mystery.' "

" What can be happening to the English

Making Conversation

language," said Martha ; " soon it will be nothing but nouns."

" ' Oxford University Student,' " her mother read.

" Three more nouns," said Martha.

" ' Frederick Jameson Simpson.' Had you ever heard of him ? "

Martha felt that her limbs had been frozen stiff, and might drop off without her noticing.

" ' And Miss Diana Lavelle, a teacher of dancing ; in a Bloomsbury boarding-establishment. Circumstances point to suicide pact.' "

It was quite true. The simplest escape from life was the gas-oven ; but the worst thing about it for Martha, she knew almost at once, was the " pact " aspect of the suicide. No wonder he hadn't written ; and she hadn't even the satisfaction of feeling widowed. She wouldn't tell her mother she had known him. What about Mr. Lal's equal and opposite reactions ? She shut herself up all day and pretended to work. When she collected all the memories of

Making Conversation

him she had, they were very few : tea, lunch and a college dance. There had been two notes from him she hadn't kept. She racked her brains for details, and not all of them were pleasant to remember. By about 6 o'clock in the evening, she wrote a long letter to Helen and felt better.

CHAPTER XV

"IT was such a good thing, darling," said Helen next term, "that there wasn't gas laid on in the Roberts Library."

"Yes, my dear. Though I often say I wish I were dead, I don't entirely mean it."

"But I'm sure if anyone asked you to turn on the gas, you would hate to refuse."

It was an enervating evening of the Summer Term. The students who slept in the garden were pulling their mattresses into place, and clattering tins of Keating's Powder. Nita Rubinstein came in and gave them some fudge.

"Oh, girls," she said, "I'm tickled to death about something!"

"What is it?"

"Guess!"

"Is it Sidney?"

"You can bet your life it is. He's in Europe on a business trip with Julian Wolheim, who's one of the most attractive

Making Conversation

men in the States. Gosh, that man has personality. I must have you meet him."

So they met him at a tea-party in the East J.C.R., with Nita and Sidney and Evangeline Catt, a Canadian, and two American Rhodes scholars. Nita had accumulated all the cushions she could borrow—square, round and banana-shaped —and Sidney had brought some roses and a big box of candies. He was small and blond, and wore a brown and white checked suit with a belt and leather buttons, and a red and yellow foulard tie ; but Mr. Wolheim was tall and dark, with terraces of black curls rising from his forehead, and the profile of an Assyrian, and he was dressed in black.

" Now," said Sidney, as a conversational opening, " who's going to marry the Prince of Wales ? "

No one knew.

" Girls," he said, " where's your ambition ? "

" I guess I wouldn't like to be a queen,"

Making Conversation

said Evangeline. " Think of poor Queen Alexandra ! "

" *I* should have lovers," said Nita ; and Sidney wiped his forehead.

" There's a lot of things I want to know about this country," said Mr. Wolheim. " Why does the waiter say thank you when he hands you the butter ? "

" Because he's afraid you won't say it yourself," said Helen, " and he thinks somebody ought to."

" Well, it seems an excess of servility to me. And why are there so many big spoons in England ? "

Helen said there were not, and the others giggled.

" There certainly are," he said, " in proportion to the average ice-cream."

" The sky is very grey," said Sidney. " In London I met a gentleman who told me that about one day in seven is fine and bright. So I guess that is how we came to have Sunday."

"This place is gosh-awful," said one of the American boys, "if it wasn't for the drink."

Making Conversation

" Ox-ford ? " asked Mr. Wolheim pronouncing both syllables distinctly. " But Ox-ford is so full of lovely lads. Flaming youth. That's what makes me jealous."

" Oh, you really needn't be," said Martha; and at that he directed the full force of his personality at her.

" I guess," he said, " that the girls and boys here get a pretty good time."

" I expect they do, on the whole."

" Now, why do you say you expect, when what you mean is *guess* ? "

" I don't know. The girls have to work hard, you know, or they may be sent down."

" Down where ? "

" Oh, anywhere. I mean away."

" And what do you work at ? " asked Mr. Wolheim, with a piercing glare which made him look like an advertisement of " This man will tell you all about your future."

" Philosophy," said Martha.

" Philosophy ? That's Kant and Hegel, isn't it ? The *Ding an Sich* ? "

Making Conversation

"Well, we don't start with modern philosophy, we start with Plato and Aristotle."

"O.K.," he said, putting his arm on the back of the sofa. "We'll start with Plato and Aristotle. What did they say?"

"Various things. I couldn't tell you all in a minute."

"That's a shame. But perhaps you could drop in and tell me another time. We might make a date."

"In Oxford?"

"Why no, in London. It's no distance, is it?"

"We aren't supposed to go away by train, you know."

"But, my dear, you wouldn't need a train to go a little way like that. You could drive up in time to have breakfast with me any morning."

"Not breakfast," said Martha firmly; "lunch."

"O.K. Lunch on Thursday at the Riviera Hotel?"

"All right. Lunch on Thursday."

Making Conversation

" Darling," said Helen afterwards, "have you ever been to the Riviera ? "

" No, have you ? "

" Of course not."

" Listen. If I miss my train that night, will you ruffle my bed to look as if I'd slept in it ? "

" Of course. But you won't miss it, will you ? "

" Of course I won't."

She had agreed to Thursday because there were cheap fares that day between Oxford and London ; and far from coming in a car, as Mr. Wolheim expected, she came on a third-class excursion ticket. The station at Oxford was crowded, and she was terrified that some woman don might be visiting the British Museum on the cheap. As the train came in she clung to the door of a carriage and secured a corner seat. Who was that woman who came in next, with a round straw hat on top of her head, like Mrs. Noah ? Could she be a tutor of the Home Students, or was she only the woman who collected for the

Making Conversation

Lifeboats with a bulldog? She was neither, as she was the mother of the young man who came in later, who went to Martha's lectures and was called Lancelot Bassett-Cumberledge. It was a name to remember, and his translations of Demosthenes used to be returned with the remark that "Mr. Bassett-Cumberledge shows signs of improvement."

It was well known that his mother lived with him and helped him with his work; and if he did not do well on Demosthenes, it was because exact scholarship was not her strong point. It was not true that he was going into the Church. Because he had a naturally clerical manner, people used to ask, " And when is Lancelot going to be ordained, Mrs. Bassett-Cumberledge? " And she would answer, " Ordained? Why not at all. Lancelot and I are conscientious agnostics."

At this moment, Lancelot was separated from her by a number of young Jewesses with short skirts and silk stockings, who kept a hat-shop and were going to London

Making Conversation

to replenish it. Elizabeth Spragge had been a customer of theirs. As he followed them, his mother glared and said, " Dear, dear ! This is what always happens to men. They are too polite, and are always *put upon*." The Jewesses giggled and made room for him.

" How's Miss Spragge ? " they asked Martha.

" She isn't here any more. She was sent down, you know. Sent away."

" What a shame ! Whatever for ? "

" Oh, for not working hard enough."

" And for going about with boys ? "

" Yes, more or less."

" I suppose you often run up to town, don't you ? "

" Pretty often," she lied.

She thought them much nicer than Lancelot, who was now writing a letter on a small block of Basildon Bond notepaper. When he had finished, he handed it to his mother to read.

" Lancelot ! " she exclaimed. "Not IE, dear ! EI ! "

Making Conversation

"Yes, mamma."

"Now, dear, on our arrival, shall we go to the Bank first, or to Uncle John's?"

"I think to the Bank," said Lancelot.

"No," said his mother, "I think we should go to Uncle John's."

Martha took a 'bus to the Riviera Hotel, and looked out of the window all the way, in case she might miss it. When she asked for Mr. Wolheim, an imposing official told her to telephone, and a boy led her to a booth. Oddly enough, she had never seen this kind of telephone before, but only the kind that wound up, and she was terrified that it would not work. His voice came through, however—a beautiful resonant American voice that sounded better on a telephone than any European one. "Good morning, my dear, would you mind coming up? I went to a party last night, and I don't feel too good."

She went up in a lift, past more floors than she could count (this must be like America), and found him in a smallish room brilliantly illuminated, with the

Making Conversation

blinds drawn. He was very pale, and wore a dressing-gown of purple brocade.

"You see," he explained, "I was a dry man for many years, but since last night I can't honestly say I am that any longer."

Martha expressed sympathy, and said it was probably a touch of influenza. He sat with his head in his hands.

"Now, a child like you," he said, "I suppose you were never burned in your life."

"Burned?"

"Yes, burned, boiled, lit up like a Christmas tree?"

"Oh, I see. No, not very badly, only slightly."

"Oh, my God! What it is to have your life in front of you. Parties! Getting burned! Well, it's worth it. Light and colour. Those are the only things that amount to anything."

"It depends where you find them," said Martha, and knew that she had been priggish. It was a remark that Gladys Parker might have made. "I mean it's

Making Conversation

rather subjective. Some people might have different colour-senses from others."

He guessed she was right, he said, and asked if she would mind having lunch upstairs. She protested that she wasn't at all hungry, and didn't want anything if he didn't. He rang a bell and ordered two Dry Martinis, a double one for himself and a single for her; and then *hors d'œuvres*, an American steak with salad, and ice-cream and iced water. As they drank the Martinis he showed her some snapshots of his children, Alfred and Clotilde, in knickerbockers and Fair Isle jumpers.

"Those are my kids," he said. "Now, everyone has to find his or her job in life, and my job is to be a pretty good parent."

Martha remarked that the little girl was very pretty.

"Clotilde," he said, " is going to have a latchkey as soon as she knows how to use it. And if she doesn't use it to put some light and colour into her life, I'm going to know the reason why."

" And what about Alfred ? "

Making Conversation

"Well, I'd like little Alfred to be a biologist or a bacteriologist or something like that. Something removed from the stress and turmoil of modern life. I'd never put him into the business."

Lunch did not arrive, and he rang a bell again. The waiter appeared to know no language, least of all American, though the hotel catered for American tourists. Mr. Wolheim ordered two more cocktails while lunch was coming.

"What is the business?" asked Martha.

"Publicity," he said. "Advertising. I reckon I'm the first all-round publicity expert in the States, though there's one fellow who's a specialist on soft drinks who's possibly better on that line."

"Do you mean to say you do nothing but advertising?"

"'Nothing but advertising'? My dear girl, would you ask Shakespeare if he did nothing but play-writing and Jesus Christ if He did nothing but preaching?"

"I'm very sorry. I hadn't thought of advertising in that way."

Making Conversation

" Why, advertising is absolutely pivotal in the modern world. Why do all the women of America and Europe, and plenty in the other continents as well, read these nice American magazines ? "

" I don't know, I'm sure."

" Why, because they're an advertisement-carrying proposition. They read these short stories by famous authors, because the famous authors have dam well got to turn them out the right size to fit between two columns of high-class advertising matter, beautifully illustrated and colour-printed."

At last the waiter brought them some pickled red cabbage.

" Do you advertise this ? " asked Martha.

" Surely. We make a very special line of canned goods. Now, I have a staff of several hundred college graduates, who are experts in literature, history, economics, art and psychology. If you want to come down to bedrock, you must go after psychology, and in publicity it's the psychology of the group mind."

Making Conversation

" I see."

" Now, the group mind is modern democracy. Do you know what happened in the States some years back, when there was a printers' strike and there were no illustrated journals ? "

" No, I'm afraid not."

"Why, the sales in all the big stores went down by seventy-five per cent., because no one knew what to buy. Publicity is the guide, philosopher and friend of modern democracy."

" Wouldn't people buy bread and butter and meat when they were hungry ? "

" No, my dear. Not under the complicated organisation of modern life. It's a more complex fabric than you know. Look at modern business. Look at the courses in commerce they have in the up-to-date universities. Look at economics."

She said, " Yes," and felt rather ill after the journey, two cocktails, red cabbage and no lunch.

" This is my thesis," he said. " Publicity bears the same relation to economics that

Making Conversation

æsthetics does to ethics. It's the æsthetics of business. I wrote a little bro-chure on the subject which you might find interesting."

"I'm sure I would," she said. Then she jumped as he suddenly banged his fist on the table and shouted, "I don't care if I smash!" The table, which was small and unsteady, shook for some time.

"Oh, but you won't, will you?" she said.

"No, I won't. But I don't care if I do. Oh, my God!"

She had never been more effectively silenced.

"Oh, my God," he said again, "I wish I were articulate."

She thought he was, almost too much so.

"Now, my dear," he said, "let's not talk any more about big business. I've always considered myself as a pretty good proletarian."

She tried not to look incredulous. "What about staying in this hotel?" she said.

"It's the only hotel in the town that

Making Conversation

offers the minimum advantages you would get at home. And it's a pretty rotten hotel at that."

She agreed. The steak had not come yet.

"I repeat," he said, "I'm a pretty good proletarian. I wouldn't care if I lost everything. Let's talk about Russia."

They talked about Russia, and the steak arrived.

"What you want," he said, "is a radical intelligentsia."

"The Russians made short work of their intelligentsia, didn't they?" said Martha.

"Did they? I don't know. I'm not interested in detail. It's only the broad issues that matter. There isn't time for anything else. Now, there's biology. You've studied biology, I suppose?"

"I'm afraid not."

"Do you mean to say they don't teach biology at Oxford?"

"Oh, they do, but everyone doesn't learn it."

"Well, that's a great pity. If you don't

Making Conversation

pay attention to biology, your studies are one-sided. Now, ethics should be scientific. Based on biology. But in the laws of every country but Russia they're not. They're based on taboo."

Martha giggled a little at the word. "Laugh if you like," he said, "but it's the superstitious dread of the medicine-man. That's what religion is. That's what stops us from leading lives that are biologically full."

"I hate science," she said. "I always did, especially experiments."

"But, my dear girl," he said, "it's scientific method that we all want. My way is to put human nature into a test-tube. Do you get me? You may call it psychology just as well. Every head of a department in my firm has to have a working knowledge of modern psychology, psycho-analysis and relativity. But biology, what was I saying about biology?"

"About leading full lives."

"That's it. You see, the male of the human species is biologically polygamous."

Making Conversation

" Is it really ? And what about the female ? "

" Oh, the female tends to be monogamous."

There was a knock at the door, and a messenger appeared with a bunch of crimson roses. " How lovely ! " said Martha.

" ' Lovely ' ? " said Mr. Wolheim. "You don't know what that means ! My God ! "

" What is it ? "

" The women of London," he said, " are cheaper than a bargain-counter. These are from a woman who wants something."

" She must have paid a lot for them," said Martha. " But do you mean she doesn't tend to be monogamous ? "

His head was in his hands again. " Shall I put them in water ? " she asked, and he didn't answer. She took them into the bathroom and put them in the basin, and when she came back, his eyes were shut. He was asleep.

Martha sat down and lighted a cigarette.

Making Conversation

Poor Mr. Wolheim, she was really sorry for him. Life and science and psychology were too much for him, and there was nothing she could do except keep still. He seemed to have a genuine interest in philosophy, and he looked so tired. She hoped none of his women friends would call. After forty minutes he woke up and stretched, and she said she ought to go home; but he gripped her by both wrists and made her sit down again. " Let's go to the pictures," he said, " and then you'll have dinner with me, won't you ? "

Dinner in London was too exciting to be missed. She remembered that Americans didn't like tea; but he rang for two more cocktails. Then he changed from the dressing-gown to his coat; and when he was in his shirt-sleeves and braces, like something in the movies, she admired his figure. As they went into the lift and out of it, out of the hotel and across the crowded London street, he took her arm in an American fashion that amused and pleased her. What would happen if they

Making Conversation

met anyone from Oxford? They found a picture-house and watched a bad historical film. He held her hand as spontaneously as he had taken her arm. On the screen a number of American he-men, with massive jaws and wreaths on their heads, were lying on couches and representing a Roman orgy. They were drinking from small medicine-glasses, and embracing baby vamps in shoulder-straps.

"I would love to attend a real orgy," said Martha.

"I could show you plenty," said Mr. Wolheim. "New York has taken the place of Vienna as the home of genuinely refined luxury."

"Then I'd love to go to New York."

But as they came out, she said she must catch the 8.30 from Paddington, and they went to a place in Shaftesbury Avenue which advertised "Theatre Dinners." He said he felt much better, and ordered champagne.

"Now, tell me all about yourself," he said.

Making Conversation

None had ever said that to her before, and it was fatal. She told him about school, and the paying-guests, and the war and Oxford, and he refilled her glass attentively.

"I suppose you've never been in love," he said.

"Of course I have," she said; "several times." And she was giving him a slightly romanticised account of Henry Butts, when she looked at a clock, and it was a quarter to nine.

She felt a pang of terror which, though deadened by alcohol, was still intense; and she knew that if she cried, he would think she was drunk. "Never mind," he said, "I'll run you home, I've been over that little bit of road before."

He was very kind, and she was almost hypnotised into taking an American view of the distance. They went back to the hotel for his car, which was long and sumptuous. It seemed hours before they were out of London. Once they were in the country, he put one arm around her

Making Conversation

shoulders and drove with the other hand, and she was afraid his efficiency would be impaired; but she could not protest, and lay quietly thinking of nothing but speed. Everything had faded from her mind but the question of getting back. Just as she thought they must be getting near Oxford, he slowed down and said, " I guess we're on the wrong road."

" Oh, do let's go on anyway," she said, and that made him stop altogether.

" Why do the roads in this country go so crooked ? " he asked in fury.

" I don't know. I can't help it; don't blame me."

" It's a quarter of eleven now," he said, " and you can't get in to-night."

" If you could get to Oxford," she said, " I might climb in. Perhaps I could get a 'bus."

" Get out and walk if you care to."

" Perhaps I will," she said, and started to get out.

" Perhaps this and perhaps that ! " he said, holding her down firmly. " Do you

Making Conversation

know that I haven't even kissed you yet?"

"Of course I know it," she snapped.

"Do you know that you're riddled with repressions and inhibitions?"

"I don't know."

"You're a living mass of them. Do you know that it isn't decent to hold a man's hand, and have him go to sleep on your shoulder, and then get out of the car because you think he wants to kiss you?"

"I don't know."

"Do you know I don't even *want* to kiss you now?"

"I don't care," she said, and burst into tears.

"I've a good mind to let you walk, after all," he said. "But we'll see what the next place is we're coming to."

It was not Oxford, but Beaconsbury, a town of the Chilterns, with a market-place surrounded by half-timbered, Gothic-lettered hotels. They stopped at one of them which was brightly lighted, and a porter opened the door of the car and said, "Luggage, sir?"

Making Conversation

" Is there a train to Oxford to-night," asked Martha.

" No, madam."

" Or a 'bus ? "

" No, madam ; the last 'bus has gone."

" Then we'd much better stop here to-night," said Mr. Wolheim. " This is a beautiful old-world place."

" I can't possibly," said Martha, and the hall-porter waited.

" Well, I've told you I don't want to kiss you," said Mr. Wolheim ; and her humiliation was complete.

" All right," she said.

" Two bedrooms," he said to the porter, who remarked that as they hadn't any luggage, they would have to pay in advance.

He said it would be £3, and did not ask them to register. It seemed expensive for the accommodation provided. Martha found cold water in the jug on her washstand, but smuts had settled on the surface during the day, and she could not bring herself to wash in it. She hung her coat in a large and heavy wardrobe ; and there was

Making Conversation

another large mahogany piece of furniture, which looked like a sideboard and might be a boot-cupboard ; and a fantastic dressing-table and chest-of-drawers. It was the first time she had ever gone to bed in her clothes and without a toothbrush ; and she lay outside the bedclothes not expecting to sleep. She thought of how much she hated Mr. Wolheim, and how much she had liked him in the afternoon. Would she get back to college before anyone found out ? If she was found out, would she be sent down ? She imagined the interview with Miss Gregory.

Towards the morning she slept a little, woke and skimmed the smuts from the water and washed her face. When she went downstairs, she expected the staff to snigger, but they took no particular notice. There was a 'bus to Oxford at 9 o'clock, they said.

CHAPTER XVI

IN her pigeon-hole at Springfield, Martha found a note from Miss Gregory's secretary summoning her to an interview; but she went to see Helen first.

"I ruffled your bed," said Helen, "but they might have found out through the porter. What happened?"

"It was all because I started talking at dinner. And then we had a row on the way back."

"You do have bad luck with your young men. You must be tactless."

The interview was exactly as Martha had feared. No, she admitted, she had not spent last night in college. Why not? She had gone to London.

"I see your name," said Miss Gregory "on the list of students who proposed to read last night in the Radcliffe Camera."

"Yes, I put it down before I went. I wasn't sure——" This was an obvious lie.

Making Conversation

" And did you spend last night in London, Miss Freke ? "

" No, not exactly ; between Oxford and London. You see, I meant to come back, but I missed my train, and the car broke down."

" Where ? "

" I'm not quite sure. Oh, yes. Beaconsbury."

" I see. And you were with friends ? "

" Oh, yes."

" Where are they ? "

" I don't know."

" Please, Miss Freke, this is important. I should like to communicate with them."

" Oh, no. I'm afraid that is impossible."

" Then I must communicate with your mother," said Miss Gregory, after a pause.

Mrs. Freke wired that she could not come to Oxford, but that Martha was to come home at once. She wondered if she should pack everything, but in the end she left Helen her cushions and Alexander the Great.

" What a shame, dear," said Mrs. Freke,

Making Conversation

as she met her at the station; " but we must make the best of it."

For the first time, Martha saw life stretching quite featureless in front of her, without any division into term and holidays.

" It's rather awkward just now," her mother went on, " as I'm thinking of getting married again."

" What ? " said Martha weakly. Here was another feature of life fading.

" Yes, I'm divorcing your father and am going to marry Shama Lal."

" But you couldn't go and live in India, could you ? "

" No, we shall stay in Europe, and spend a lot of time on the Riviera."

" How lovely ! "

" We shall be able to give you an allowance."

The College Council interviewed Martha's tutors, who reported her to be idle and immature. Her philosophy tutor said her interests were more literary than philosophic ; and her history tutor said

Making Conversation

she had no idea of historical method. So they gave her place to the " better woman " who was waiting for it.

" Can I go and live in London ? " Martha asked her mother.

" You can go there if you can get something to do, dear."

" But I can't get anything to do unless I go there first."

" Uncle Randolph," said Mrs. Freke, " could get you a job in Czecho-Slovakia, teaching English to a family. Prague is a beautiful city. But I should always be afraid of wars breaking out in the Balkans."

" It isn't the Balkans. You're think of Jugo-Slavia."

" Well, it's much the same. These new countries are so difficult. And I believe the Czechs all insist on talking Czech."

" I suppose that's rather natural."

" Most foreigners," said Mrs. Freke, " will talk French or German. But Uncle Randolph says he knows a very nice family. And the exchange is in our favour."

Martha sent for a Czech phrase-book.

Making Conversation

It started by giving the Lord's Prayer in every Slavonic language, including Old Slavonic and Lusatian Serbian. This might not be much use to the traveller; but it was followed by the encouraging statement that if a Bohemian learned Russian thoroughly, he would then be able to understand the remaining Slavonic languages with a certain degree of accuracy. (How amusing that they were called Bohemians.) Next it was admitted that there were thirty-nine letters in the alphabet, and that nouns had seven cases. What a judgment on her for neglecting Greek and Latin, which were easy languages! The phrasebook finally revealed itself as especially suitable for Czech immigrants in America. " How long have you been in America ? " " Have you a cough ? " " Have you spat blood ? " " What wages do you get ? " " Do you suffer from rheumatism (neuritis, neuralgia, asthma, sciatica) ? "

But as she set off from Victoria Station, Martha felt it was wonderful to be going to a fresh country, even a new

Making Conversation

country, where no one would bother about Oxford.

"Don't get into conversation with anyone on the journey," said her mother.

"I'll never get into conversation with anyone again," she said; and recognised that she had a certain English fear that foreigners would be lecherous.

It was a fine day, and the boat from Folkestone to Flushing was not crowded. A sailor proposed to put her chair in the sunshine, next to a fat gentleman in a tweed cap, whom she took to be a dangerous Central European. "No, not there," she said, and chose another place, where she applied herself to a little book called *All you want in Holland*. She would have to face the Dutch Customs, but Dutch was easier than Czech. "I have nothing to declare" was, phonetically speaking, "*Ick hepp nits ter* . . ." and then something harder.

A voice said, "Did you think I'd bite you?" It was the fat man, who had moved his chair; but the voice was unmistakably

Making Conversation

English, with a suggestion of cockney.

" Not at all," she said coldly.

" Lovely day," he said.

" Lovely."

" Know this trip well ? "

What a pitfall, she thought; and said, " Not very."

" I know it pretty well myself. I'm living in Dresden now."

" Really ? "

" Yes, I'm just moving over some of my goods and chattels."

She did not answer.

" Don't care for it much myself. But it's for business reasons."

" I see."

" Beggars can't be choosers, can they ? "

" I suppose not."

"I've got the wife and kids out there, too."

" Really ? "

" Like to see the paper," he asked, meaning the *Daily Mail*.

" No, thank you, I've seen it."

" No, I don't care for living out of

Making Conversation

England. A little place in the country, that's what I should like. A bit of gardening, and playing the organ in the village church, and dropping in for a bit of a chat with the vicar now and again. That would suit me."

" Oh, really ? "

" Yes, the organ's my hobby. Look here, what *are* you ? "

She started and said, " What do you mean ? "

" Church or chapel ? "

" Oh, Church, I suppose."

" Well, which do you use—*Hymns A. and M.* or *The Hymnal Companion* ? "

" *The Hymnal Companion*," she said.

" I'm glad to hear it." And he began looking in his note-case and said, " I've got some snaps of my kids here, playing with some German kiddies."

The English had forgiven the Germans now, it seemed ; but Martha was on her guard against business men who had snapshots of their children.

" They're picking up the lingo, too," he

Making Conversation

said. " It's wonderful what kids will pick up. Now, I've been looking for someone to sign this paper about my furniture. I'm taking over some rugs with me this time, and I've got to prove they're my own property. Will you sign here and say you know me ? " He handed her another paper from his note-case.

" Oh, but I couldn't possibly," she said.

" Come on ! It won't do you any harm. I've been looking round for somebody English to do me a good turn, and all the other passengers on this boat seem to be foreigners."

" I don't see why I should," said Martha.

" Look here," said the fat man, to a man on his other side, " can *you* do anything for me ? Do you speak German ? "

Yes, he did. He was a young man in a black felt hat, with a navy-blue belted mackintosh, and carried what looked like a music-case. He could not be English.

" If you could do anything for me with the Customs——" said the fat man, and

Making Conversation

began to explain again about the rugs, while Martha fled.

As she was looking at the sea the young man in the black hat approached and said, " Your husband seems to be upset."

She burst into laughter and said, " He's not my husband."

" You are both English ? "

" Yes, I am English, but I can't help that. I hate the English."

" I am an internationalist," he said. " I have no national hatreds."

" Do you think that man is a crook ? "

" Possibly not. Only very stupid."

Another man in a mackintosh came and spoke an unintelligible language to the black-hatted man, who turned his back.

" Was that another crook ? " asked Martha.

" No, it is a Czech. You see, I am a Czech. And if there is one race I cannot stand, it is the Czechs."

" Really, I thought they must be very nice. I'm going to Czecho-Slovakia."

" What for ? "

Making Conversation

" To teach English in a family."

" Then I pity you."

" Why, what are they like ? "

" Dull. Very dull."

" But I thought they would be exciting after a revolution and everything."

" After a revolution, people are not exciting. I like the English, they have a good literature. Shaw and Wells." (He pronounced them Shav and Vells.)

The bell rang for lunch, and they went downstairs together, while the fat man eyed them with disgust.

" The English are an enlightened people," said the Czech.

" Not at all. They are most conventional," said Martha.

" But the young English, in the universities ? "

" The universities are strongholds of convention."

As they ate a large Dutch meal they discussed the part played by students in political life ; and after lunch they watched a Dutchman, who had taken two helpings

Making Conversation

of soup, fish and meat, insert himself with difficulty into a lifebelt. The boat was not sinking, but he was preparing to sleep, and taking no risks.

"Are you going to Prague?" asked the Czech.

"Yes."

"Then I shall come to see you. What is your address?"

This was just what she had been warned against, but she gave it to him all the same. At Flushing he helped her with her luggage, and found her place in the train. They met at dinner, and he told her that thirty-three and a third per cent. of the Czech nation was in the service of the Government. Yes, she was going to the family of a Government official, Mr. Karel Hamak.

"They consider themselves the best nation in the world," he said, "and in the universe, including the other planets. There is very much *chauvinisme*."

"But haven't they a lot of modern art and concerts?"

Making Conversation

" Yes. That is for the tourists. Have you any money ? "

She looked at her handbag nervously, and said, " A little."

" Good," he said.

That night she shared a sleeper with a German lady, who had brought her own sheets and pillow-cases, and wore a nightcap. When one thought of germs, how dangerous life was ; but it was exciting to rush through these foreign countries in the train.

At breakfast her friend told her that his name was Josef Bumbrlička, and that he was an engineer ; that his mother told him he ought to marry and settle down ; but that much as he disliked Czech men, he disliked Czech women more. The fat Englishman ate fried eggs and bacon ; and as they stood in the corridor afterwards and smoked, he came up and said, " That was the best breakfast I ever had. Can you tell me when lunch comes on ? "

" They will tell you," said Josef.

" Look here," he said, " I can't

Making Conversation

understand the lingo. Will you tell the fellow I want one ticket?"

At lunch they heard another English voice, which made Martha jump and reminded her of Oxford. "My dear sir," it said, "surely you remember that the last years of Justinian were embittered by the incursion of Slavs into the Peloponnese?"

It was evidently a don at the next table. It might have been Mr. Barrington-Ramsbotham, but it wasn't.

"How many?" asked a thick German voice.

"Why, several millions."

"What did they live on?" asked the German. "Did they bring their *food* with them?"

"The only way to keep fit in Greece," said the don later, "is to have a bowl of those curds—I forget what they call them—the first thing every morning. Not for breakfast, that's no use, but as soon as you wake."

At Prague, Martha said good-bye to Josef, and was met by Mrs. and Miss

Making Conversation

Hamak. They looked kind, but less Slavonic than she had hoped. " I guess you had a long trip," said Mrs. Hamak nasally —she must have learned English from an American, but her vocabulary was small. The daughter grinned and said nothing; she was wearing a béret and a Central-European tweed coat, and brown stockings and black shoes.

They took her to a large flat in the suburbs, and on the way they all agreed that Prague was a beautiful city. Martha was sorry to see that their interior decoration was not ultra-modern; but there was an excellent supper of ham and sausages and different kinds of bread. " To-morrow," said Mrs. Hamak, smiling, " you shall show us English national dishes." (Good God, would she have to cook?)

Mr. Hamak was a severe gentleman with a tight black coat and a stiff collar. " You must see our city," he said, slowly and with difficulty. " Prague is a beautiful city."

" Of course. A very beautiful city."

Making Conversation

"You have read history? *Vous avez lu l'histoire de la Tchéquo-Slovakie?*"

"*Oui, un peu.*"

"Then you know the Bohemian language, *la langue bohémienne*, was *autrefois la langue diplomatique de toute l'Europe*, of all the Europe."

"Oh, really?"

"At the present, the cultural standard is high. We have a small proportion of analphabets."

She said, "How splendid!" and they allowed her to go to bed. The next morning, a letter was delivered for her by hand. It was more than she had hoped; but it could be from no one but Josef Bumbrlička. He addressed her as You with a capital letter, as if she were God.

"DEAR MISS FREKE," he said—"I hope You are well after Your journey. I hope to see You again, and will say at once that I have found You sympathetic. I wish to make to You a proposal. I often wished to marry an English woman of

Making Conversation

English education, and for that I would risk occasional indigestion. I do not wish to marry a housewife, as Bohemian women are. Also I will not hide from You that it is good to have money, as our exchange has lowered. I think that physical attraction is not a basis for marriage, but intellectual sympathy and financial convenience are better. Please tell me if You do not agree with this idea. If You do, please tell me where I can see You."

What a chance, she thought. Nowhere but here would she be a good match; and he was delightfully candid. It was good for her to learn the Czech language, and until then, to speak simple, distinct English. Never again would her tongue run away with her, and she would change her character with her nationality. It was worth trying; and she wrote, " I am prepared to consider your idea."

THE END

If you have enjoyed this Persephone book why not telephone or write to us for a free copy of the *Persephone Catalogue* and the current *Persephone Biannually*? All Persephone books ordered from us cost £12 or three for £30 plus £2 postage per book.

PERSEPHONE BOOKS LTD
59 Lamb's Conduit Street
London WC1N 3NB

Telephone: 020 7242 9292
sales@persephonebooks.co.uk
www.persephonebooks.co.uk